TWEAK TH

Driving to the El Patio club to see his girlfriend Fausta Moreni, the establishment's proprietor, private investigator Manville Moon does not expect to be witness to a murder. As he steps from his car outside the club, he hears a gun suddenly roar from the bushes close behind him. Walter Lancaster, the lieutenant governor of the neighbouring state of Illinois, has been shot! The assassination will not only make headlines all over the country, but also place the lives of Moon and Fausta in deadly danger . . .

Books by Richard Deming
in the Linford Mystery Library:

THE GALLOWS IN MY GARDEN

RICHARD DEMING

◆

TWEAK THE DEVIL'S NOSE

Complete and Unabridged

LINFORD
Leicester

First published in Great Britain

First Linford Edition
published 2016

A catalogue record for this book is available
from the British Library.

ISBN 978–1–4448–2914–3

Published by
F. A. Thorpe (Publishing)
Anstey, Leicestershire

Set by Words & Graphics Ltd.
Anstey, Leicestershire
Printed and bound in Great Britain by
T. J. International Ltd., Padstow, Cornwall

This book is printed on acid-free paper

DEDICATION
For Alys, who watched over
my shoulder.

1

There are two reasons I like the El Patio club as an occasional dining spot. It serves the finest food within a fifty-mile radius, and its proprietress is Fausta Moreni. It is also the last place in the world you would expect to witness a murder, though this was not a factor in my preference when I passed up three alternate dining places I like in favor of El Patio on the July evening Walter Lancaster was assassinated.

Actually it had been the scene of a murder once before, but that was back in its days as a gambling casino, when its atmosphere was more conducive to homicide. Since Fausta had taken it over, eliminated the gaming tables and built it a reputation based on food, it had become the quietest supper club in town.

El Patio was originally named, I imagine, by someone who liked the sound of the words but knew no Spanish, for there is nothing within sight of it even faintly resembling a courtyard. It is a huge gray stone building of two stories, from the outside resembling a prison. But inside it is magnificent: three enormous rooms run nearly the width of the building from front to rear; and as you enter through the heavy bronze double doors (a holdover from its casino days when the place sometimes had to be barricaded against invading cops), you find yourself in a cocktail lounge so glittering you automatically brace yourself to pay double the normal rate for drinks.

To the left of the cocktail lounge an archway leads to the ballroom, where a five-dollar cover charge gets you a table, authorizes you to watch a floor show so sedate it would pass the scrutiny of a Methodist convention, and permits you to dance on a floor actually large enough to accommodate the usual crowd. It is the only night club I have ever been in which offers the twin innovations of entertainment, without smutty jokes and naked women, and sufficient room to dance.

To the right a similar archway leads to the dining room, billed by Fausta as 'The

Dining Place of Kings' ever since a deposed monarch stopped for a sandwich when he was motoring through the city a few years back. It is the dining room which brings Fausta her fortune. Not that she loses on either of the other rooms, for both draw as well as can be expected in a town which does not particularly go for night-club life. But seven nights a week the dining room is packed to the walls.

Yet oddly enough the club is out of the way and inconvenient to reach. Isolated in the center of a three-acre patch of ground at the extreme south edge of town, and on a secondary highway, you would hardly expect it to draw the crowds it does, for though its location was logical for a gambling casino, it is about as poor as can be imagined for a night club. But in this case the old adage about a better mousetrap worked out. Customers — not the fickle night-club crowd which makes new clubs boom the first month and then suddenly deserts for a new attraction, but a solid clientele which sticks year after year — book reservations weeks in advance and come from as far as fifty miles away to keep them.

I had no reservation, however, for when you start out for dinner as late as I did this particular night, you are not likely to have trouble finding a table anywhere. It was just nine thirty when I drove between the two stone pillars marking the entrance to El Patio's drive. The drive, which runs past the club's front entrance, then angles left alongside the building to a parking lot at the rear, separates El Patio from a heavily treed park-like area some hundred yards square. This area offered excellent cover to the assassin.

Had the taxi driver who pulled into the drive immediately ahead of me behaved as drivers familiar with the place do, possibly I would not have been involved in the murder at all, but apparently he was a new driver and did not know procedure. Instead of continuing back to the lot, turning around and returning to the entrance with his nose pointed toward the highway, he slammed on his brakes in front of the steps leading up to the bronze doors, jumped out and left his cab in the center of the drive, blocking traffic both ways.

Behind him I slammed on my own brakes just in time to avoid collision, then accidentally let my toe slip off the clutch, which caused the car to jolt forward and gently clang bumpers. This happened because I operate both foot pedals with my left foot, my right being an intricate contrivance of cork and aluminum below the knee.

Shortly after the war the Veterans Administration gave me a specially built Olds in return for the leg I left overseas, a sedan with the foot brake on the left and with an attachment which caused the clutch to disengage when the brake pedal was pushed halfway down. But when I finally traded it in on a 1951 Plymouth, I could not afford the special attachments. Consequently when I brake, I turn my left foot sidewise, hitting the brake with my heel and the clutch with my toe. I have gotten pretty good at it, but this time I slipped.

The cabbie, a cocky bantamweight with a strut like a Prussian sergeant major's, stopped halfway up the steps, ran down again and anxiously stared at his undamaged bumper. Then he inquired belligerently,

'Whyn't you learn how to drive?'

'Whyn't you learn how to park?' I countered, mimicking his tone. 'Pick either side of the drive you want and I'll take the other.'

'Yeah?' he asked. 'I got a customer, bud. I'll move when I finish loading.'

As he started up the steps again, I got out of my car, swung open the driver's door of the taxi and climbed in. The motor was running, and I had pulled the cab forward and to the right so that it was flush against the shrubbery edging the driveway before the cabbie realized what was happening. 'Hey!' he yelled, starting down again.

By the time he reached me I was out of the cab and had slammed the door. Near the left rear fender he stopped me by planting both hands on hips and halting directly in my path. He was only about five feet six and weighed possibly ninety-nine pounds, but his chin was thrust out and his expression said he could handle any two guys my size.

Grinning down at him, I tried to step around, but he moved his body to block me again. At the top of the steps I was conscious of the uniformed doorman watching this maneuvering with interest, and I began to grow a little irked. I suspected if I tried to push the bantam taxi driver aside, he would swing on me, and I had no desire to fight a man half my size. At the same time I do not enjoy being shoved around even by midgets.

I was saved from a decision by the big bronze doors opening and a man in white Palm Beach stepping out. Immediately the doorman clapped his hands and called, 'Taxi for Mr. Lancaster!'

As the man descended the steps the little cabbie said darkly, 'I'll see you again, buster,' and moved to open the rear door of the taxi.

I grinned at him again, took a step toward my own car just as the white-suited man passed between me and the cabbie, then half-turned to glance back at the man as something familiar about his appearance struck me.

At that moment a gun roared so close to my ear it started bells ringing in my head.

The taxi driver, whose back had been turned while he opened the door, twisted around to gape at his customer. All three of us — the doorman, the taxi driver and I — stood transfixed as the man in white slowly spun around and collapsed on his face.

The cabbie recovered first. He gave me a horrified look and dived in front of his cab out of the line of fire. It did not occur to me at the moment that he thought I had fired the shot at him, missed and hit his customer.

As the little cabbie tried to dig a hole in the gravel drive, I swung toward the bush from which the shot had come. It was a dark night, I was unarmed, and I had no intention of trying to grapple with the gunman, so I made no attempt to rush after him. But I did listen, and I could hear the rustle of fallen leaves as someone moved hastily toward the highway.

Swiftly I ran toward my car, leaped in and threw it in reverse. My intention was to back the approximately fifty yards to the drive entrance, swing my lights along the edge of the park-like area where it touched the highway, and attempt to get a glimpse of the gunman when he reached the road. But I was foiled by another car swinging into the drive just before I reached the stone pillars.

Braking, I attempted to honk it out of the way, but the driver failed to get the point and simply sat there. Finally I jumped out and shouted, 'Emergency! Back out and let me pass!'

So what did the guy do? He got flustered and killed his engine. At the same moment I heard a car spin its wheels as it roared away from about where I figured the assassin would have come out on the road.

Giving up, I told the driver behind me to forget it, and drove back and parked behind the cab. In the interval, a number of people had come out of the club. At the top of the steps I spotted the vivid blonde hair of Fausta Moreni, flaming like a pink beacon in the light of the neon sign over the door. Surrounded by customers, she calmly listened to the doorman's excited story.

Standing over the crumpled white figure

next to the cab, a forty-five automatic in his hand, was Marmaduke Greene, affectionately known to his friends as 'Mouldy' due to a mild but persistent case of acne. Seeing me return, the cabbie had crowded behind Mouldy's wide back.

'That's him!' the cabbie hissed in Mouldy's misshapen ear. 'Look out! He's got a gun!'

Mouldy Greene's flat face registered amazement. 'Manny Moon?' he asked over his shoulder. 'The sarge tried to use a rod on a little punk like you? And missed on top of it?' He shook his gun at me in a friendly kind of way. 'Hi, Sarge. What's new?'

'Put it away,' I told him, eying the automatic warily. Mouldy is not the safest person in the world to let handle a gun, sometimes forgetting what he has in his hand and absently squeezing the trigger.

'Sure, Sarge.' Obediently he tucked it under the arm of his dinner jacket.

During World War II, Mouldy Greene had been the sad sack of my outfit overseas. Every outfit had at least one: a well-meaning bungler with a talent for

10

fouling up every detail he was assigned, but for whom you developed the same sort of exasperated fondness a mother feels for an idiot child.

Immediately after the war, while El Patio was still a gambling casino, the underworld character who owned the place hired Mouldy as a bodyguard. He must have been hard up for strong-arm men, for while Mouldy looks tough, having a build like a rhinoceros and a face nearly as flat as the top of his head, he has a mind like a rhinoceros too. He proved just as efficient a bodyguard as he had a soldier, managing to be leaning against El Patio's bar when a business rival put a bullet through his boss's head.

Fausta inherited Mouldy when she took over El Patio, and while she had no compunction about instantly firing the other gunmen and bouncers inhabiting the place as members of the club's staff, it would have taken a harder heart than Fausta possessed to cast Mouldy out into a competitive world. She tried him as a waiter, bus boy, and even as head waiter before she gave up in despair and created a special job for him.

Mouldy was official customer greeter for the establishment. Evenings he stood just inside the main entrance with a hideous smile on his face, calling celebrities by their first names (generally the wrong ones), familiarly slapping barebacked dowagers on the back, and in general acting the part of the genial host with earthy informality. The customers loved it once they got over the initial shock, and in the public mind he had become an institution.

Now he casually collared the miniature cabbie, held him with his feet dangling six inches off the ground, and asked, 'What about this guy, Sarge?' The 'Sarge' was a holdover from army days, and I had given up trying to break him of the habit.

'Put him down,' I said. 'He hasn't done anything.'

Stooping, I felt for pulse in the prone man's wrist, but found none. He was lying on his chest, both arms flung forward, and there were bloodstains immediately beneath each armpit, indicating the bullet had passed entirely through him from right to left.

The man lay on one cheek, a thin, austere-looking face turned in the direction of the club entrance. In the dim light cast by the neon sign 'El Patio' immediately over the bronze doors, I again thought I detected something familiar about his appearance, but it eluded me. I was sure I had never seen him before, but almost equally sure I had seen his picture somewhere.

'Know who he is?' I asked Mouldy.

'Butch here?' He shook his head. 'First time he's dropped in.'

'Then how do you know his name's Butch?'

'Huh? Oh, I call 'em all Butch when I don't know who they are. Sounds better than just 'Hey you!''

Ordinarily I know better than to ask Mouldy anything at all, but it had been some time since I had seen him and I was a little rusty.

To the little cabbie, who had again dodged behind Mouldy as soon as his collar was released and was still peering at me apprehensively, I said, 'Shut off your motor and prepare to stick around. The cops will want you as a witness.'

As an afterthought I told Mouldy to keep track of the little man until the police arrived. Then I walked over to the steps, which were by now packed by at least twenty people. Others, still half-inside, held wide the big double doors, and behind them crowded a solid pack of customers straining to see what was going on. For some reason, possibly because the door-man, like the cabbie, had the impression I was the one who had fired the shot and had passed his opinion along, no one but Mouldy had ventured further than the lowest step. The manner in which the crowd seemed to shrink back as I neared substantiated this guess.

I had never thought my experience as a first sergeant during the war would be of any value in civilian life, but after all the intervening years I finally found a use for one thing I had learned. Summoning up my old parade-ground voice, I boomed, 'Everybody back to their tables! *On the double!*'

The whole crowd jumped like people do after a thunder crash. Then they meekly turned and filed back inside, leaving only Fausta and the doorman on the steps. The doorman eyed me nervously and seemed inclined to follow the customers inside where there were no homicidal maniacs running loose.

Fausta turned her big brown eyes on me. 'What happened, Manny?'

'In a minute, Fausta,' I said. I looked at the doorman, an imposing figure in the maroon uniform of a Central American general. 'Seems to me you called yonder corpse by name. Who is he?'

He swallowed and finally got out, 'Mr. Walter Lancaster, sir.'

My hair nearly turned white. Being innocently involved in a murder is bad enough. Having one witness, and possibly two, convinced you are the killer is even worse. But when the victim is the kind whose assassination will cause deep-seated political repercussions and make headlines all over the country, you are, to put it mildly, in an unpleasant spot.

Walter Lancaster was lieutenant governor of our neighboring state, Illinois.

2

At twenty-seven, Fausta Moreni is one of the richest women in the city, but when I first met her during the war she was a nineteen-year-old penniless refugee from fascist Italy, frightened and alone in a strange country. Most of America's Italian immigrants have come from Sicily and southern Italy, but Fausta was from Rome. While she is as dark-eyed as her southern countrywomen, her skin is a creamy tan instead of the sultry olive possessed by most southern Italian beauties, and her hair is a gleaming natural blonde.

Fascinated partly by her Latin explosiveness and comic-opera accent, and partly by what I took to be her defenselessness in an alien land, I went overboard for her like a moonstruck teenager in spite of having attained the sophisticated age of twenty-four. All during the war I carried her picture in my pocket and a vague plan for a vine-covered cottage in my heart.

But when I finally returned from overseas plus a long period in a V.A. hospital, nearly five years had passed and Fausta had outgrown my mental image. Only traces of her accent lingered, and in place of a naïve and dependent teenager I found an assured young career woman well on her way to parlaying her culinary genius into a fortune. When I recovered from the shock, I found I was just as much attracted to her as ever, but I no longer felt like much of a catch.

Fausta insisted it made no difference who had the money, the husband or wife, but it did to me. I will not try to defend my position. I admit I am pigheaded, arrogantly proud, unrealistic and all the other things well-meaning friends, including Fausta, have told me I am for refusing to marry the woman. But that is what I did.

We seldom see each other now, but I have never been able to get very excited over any other woman, and Fausta has never indicated matrimonial interest in any of the numerous men who chase her. Though long ago we tacitly dropped the subject of marriage, it pleases her to pretend she pursues me hotly, and to go along with the game I make a pretense of trying to struggle off the hook.

We waited in Fausta's office for the police to arrive. Before phoning, I had Fausta announce to the crowd what had happened and request that no one leave until released by the police. To insure compliance she posted waiters at the front door and each of the two side entrances with instructions to be firm. She also asked if there was a doctor in the house, and when it developed there were three, I sent them all out to hold a consultation over the corpse, first requesting them not to disturb the body beyond what was necessary to verify that Lancaster was actually dead. They decided he was.

Instead of phoning headquarters I phoned Inspector Warren Day at his bachelor apartment, getting the reaction I anticipated. 'Listen, Moon,' he growled, 'headquarters is full of cops. Why bother me when I'm off duty?'

'This one is too hot for anybody less than the chief of Homicide,' I told him. 'I've got the lieutenant governor of Illinois laid out for you.'

He was silent a minute. Then he asked querulously, 'You're kidding, aren't you?'

'No.'

He took a deep breath and blistered my ear with profanity. 'A political assassination! Plain murder's not fancy enough. You got to give me a political assassination!'

'I didn't shoot him,' I said reasonably.

'Wouldn't put it past you,' he snarled. 'Don't let anybody go. Be there in fifteen minutes.'

When I hung up Fausta said in a small voice, 'Tom says you shot that man, Manny.'

'Tom?'

'The doorman. He said he saw it.'

'He saw an optical illusion,' I told her. 'I never commit my murders in front of witnesses.'

Her brow puckered in concentration. 'I could tell him not to say anything in front of the police, but he told it in front of all

19

those customers on the steps.' Then she brightened. 'I was outside when the shooting happened. I had just left the side door from the ballroom and was walking around to the front entrance for a breath of air. I will say I stepped out to meet you and we were making love in the bushes when the shot sounded. Then the police will think it must have been another person he saw.'

'I didn't shoot the guy,' I said irritably. 'Someone fired from behind a bush right next to me. Incidentally, I came out here for dinner, but once the cops get here it may be hours before I get a chance to eat. How about rustling up a fast sandwich?'

'Food!' Fausta said. 'You shoot a man and it makes you hungry? I should think instead you would want to kiss me goodbye before they take you off to jail.'

She looked at me expectantly and I said, 'Roast beef if you've got it. And a cup of coffee.'

'You are a corpse yourself,' she said without heat, and lifted her desk phone to order.

I was munching on the sandwich when

the police arrived. Minutes before they got there we heard the sirens in the distance, and they grew to a scream as they reached the drive entrance, then faded away to a final snarl. When I figured they were entering the front door, I took my sandwich in one hand and my coffee in the other and followed Fausta out to the dining room.

We arrived just as Inspector Warren Day, trailed by his silent satellite, Lieutenant Hannegan, and two uniformed cops, entered the dining room through the arch from the cocktail lounge. Day's spare figure, attired in a shapeless seersucker suit, halted just inside the archway. Ducking his skinny head to peer over thick-lensed glasses, he slowly swept his eyes over the assembled hundred or so diners until all conversation stopped. Then he suddenly jerked off his flat straw sailor to disclose a totally bald scalp.

In a booming voice he announced, 'I'm Inspector Warren Day of Homicide!' He should have made his announcement in the ballroom first, where they had an orchestra, for it would have been much more effective followed by a flurry of trumpets.

A half-dozen male customers immediately left their tables to cluster around the inspector and yammer about appointments they had to keep. Day listened for about thirty seconds, then suddenly roared, 'Shut up!'

They all stood looking at him with their mouths open. Ignoring them, the inspector glowered out over the others in the room. 'Anybody here know anything at all about this?' he inquired.

When a half-minute had passed without any volunteers stepping forward, he said, 'You'll find a cop at the door with a half-dozen notepads, so several of you can write at once. Sign your names, addresses and telephone numbers and go on home.' Then, belatedly realizing there were probably innumerable influential people in the crowd, he turned on a fierce smile which apparently he meant to be ingratiating. 'Sorry if anyone was inconvenienced,' he said grudgingly. 'We got here as fast as we could.'

As the crowd began to leave their tables and file past the inspector and his party, Day turned to snap something at Hannegan. The inscrutable lieutenant merely nodded, never being one to waste words where a gesture would serve, and left the room. I guessed Day had instructed him to repeat the performance in the other two rooms.

Then the inspector began to work his way through the crowd toward us. But halfway he stopped and grasped a dinner-jacketed man by the sleeve. The accosted man, a handsome fellow of about thirty, shrugged off the inspector's hand impatiently.

'Not so fast!' Day roared, then said something to one of the uniformed cops with him.

Scowling at the man belligerently, the cop dropped a meaty hand on his shoulder and pushed him over toward the far wall, where he fixed him with a watchful eye and simply waited. Apparently Day had instructed that the man be held until he could question him at leisure.

'Who's that?' I asked Fausta as the

inspector again began his approach.

'Barney Seldon.'

'The gangster from across the river?'

'I believe Mr. Seldon is a businessman,' she said with odd primness.

Before I could pursue the subject any further, Warren Day stopped before us and eyed me moodily. I said, 'Evening, Inspector,' put the last bite of sandwich in my mouth, and chewed it with enjoyment.

Day turned his gaze at Fausta. 'Miss Moreni, isn't it?'

There was none of the usual strain in his manner which appears when he is faced by a beautiful woman. Ordinarily he exhibits traces of psychotic terror when he has to speak to any woman at all, and the degree of terror increases in direct proportion to her beauty. Fausta's should have reduced him to a dithering wreck, but she is the exception which proves the rule. Possibly because he had met her on a number of previous occasions, but more probably because he refused to be in awe of any woman who would associate with me, she was the one woman I knew with whom he was able to be almost entirely natural.

When Fausta admitted she was Miss Moreni, Day said, 'May we use your office for questioning?'

'Certainly,' Fausta said, turning to lead the way.

Back in the office I sipped a quarter of my coffee, then set the cup in the saucer I had left on Fausta's desk. The inspector watched me with irritation.

'May I interrupt your meal long enough to ask what happened, Moon?' he inquired acidly.

'Sure, Inspector. I'll even skip my dessert. Somebody hiding in the bushes right across from the club entrance shot Lancaster just as he started to climb into a taxi.'

I explained in detail just what I knew, including my argument with the taxi driver and his apparent assumption I had been shooting at him and missed.

'The doorman thinks I shot him too,' I said.

'Did you?' he asked.

I gave him a pained look. 'You think I'd

miss and get the wrong man at a distance of four feet?'

'Maybe it was Lancaster you meant to get.' He turned to the cop who still remained with him. 'Bring in that cabbie and the doorman. And tell Lieutenant Hannegan I want him.'

While awaiting these arrivals, I went back to sipping my coffee. Fausta sat on the edge of her desk and crossed her legs, which parted a knee-high slit in the side of her green evening gown to expose a beautiful silk-clad calf. Instinctively the inspector gawked at it, then turned his head to study the far corner of the room.

The moment the little cabbie was ushered into the office by the cop Day had sent after him, he pointed a finger at me and said in a shrill voice, 'There he is! He done it!'

'What's your name?' the inspector asked in a bored tone.

'Caxton. Robert Caxton. This guy tried to kill me, but he hit that other character instead. You take away his gun?'

'Just tell your story, Caxton,' Warren Day suggested.

26

Except for implying he had left plenty of room for any normal driver to pass when he parked his cab, and stating I had no business to move his cab, the little man's story corroborated mine up to the point of the shot. From there on we were miles apart.

'As soon as he seen what he'd done, he put away his rod, jumped in his car and tried to escape by backing out the drive,' he said. 'But another car was coming in, and when he saw he couldn't make it, he come back to brazen it out.'

'You saw him put away the gun?' Day asked.

'Sure I seen him. He wasn't five feet away from me.'

'What kind of gun was it?'

'Geeze, I don't know. Everything happened too fast. I heard the shot, turned around, and there he was with this gun in his hand — '

'Turned around,' I interrupted. 'Catch that, Inspector? He was opening the door for his customer and had his back to both of us. When the shot went off, he took one look at me and dived in front of his cab. Ask him how he saw me put away a gun when he had his face in the gravel under his radiator.'

'Shut up, Moon,' the inspector said without anger. He looked up as the doorman Tom was ushered into the room by Hannegan. 'What's your name?'

'Thomas Henning, sir.'

'What's your story?'

The doorman, though less definite about it, generally verified Robert Caxton's accusation. He refused to say right out I had done the shooting, but said that was his impression. His eyes had been on Lancaster when the shot came, and a lance of flame seemed to come from where I was standing. He cheerfully admitted it could have come from the bushes, however, and his assumption I had done the shooting could have been based on the fact no one else was in evidence.

'Hmph,' the inspector said. He stared at me with relish. 'Guess we'll have to book you overnight at least, Moon.'

I glared at him. 'You know damn well this little twerp is talking through his hat, Inspector.'

'He sounds like a reliable witness to me, Moon. I hate to drag in an old friend, but I can't let friendship interfere with duty.'

He beamed at me piously as I tried to decide whether to kill him right then, or wait till I had a chance to plan out the crime so that I might get away with it. Warren Day is probably one of the best homicide cops in the country, but he is also, to put it mildly, eccentric. And one of the symptoms of his eccentricity is that he firmly believes he has a sense of humor.

He hated to drag in an old friend like I hate fresh apple pie. He had known me so long, I was sure he held no belief whatever in the possibility of my being the killer, merely seeing an excellent opportunity to exercise what he regarded as his sense of humor. Day's sense of humor is the kind which activates on fat men slipping on banana peels, or women getting their noses caught in wash wringers. It would split his sides to have me spend the night in the pokey.

Fausta said suddenly, 'Nobody asked

me who the killer was.'

Everybody in the room turned to look at her. Finally Day asked, 'Do you know?'

'I know it was not Manny,' she said positively. 'I was just coming around the corner of the building from the side door to the ballroom when the gun went off. It was a man behind a bush right next to Manny. I could see his face in the light from the neon sign.'

'Wait a minute, Fausta,' I said. 'You don't have to — '

'I cannot describe him,' she said firmly, 'because I could only see his head. I do not know whether he was thin or fat, or how tall he was, because I think he was crouched a little. But I would recognize his face if I saw it again.'

After a moment during which no one said anything, Day growled, 'You're making that up to save your boyfriend's skin. You didn't say anything about it when Moon was telling his story.'

'You did not ask me, Inspector.' She looked at him calmly. 'Many customers who saw me can testify I stepped from the ballroom door a few minutes before the shot came. I wish to make a formal statement, and I would like a copy to show the judge when he asks you why you arrested Manny.'

The inspector gave up. Had he held the slightest belief in my guilt, probably he would have thrown Fausta in the cooler as an accessory along with me. But since he had only been exercising his perverted sense of humor in the first place, he decided to let it drop.

'Take her statement, Hannegan,' he said briefly. 'Okay, Moon, you can shove off. But stay in town. Understand?'

'I was thinking of a Canadian fishing trip,' I growled back at him.

Just then a medical examiner stuck his head in the door and informed Day that Lancaster was dead. He had been for nearly an hour by then, of course, and this was the fourth doctor to say so, but this made it official.

3

By the time I got home the news of Walter Lancaster's death was on the radio and special bulletins were coming over every few minutes. Having stopped for a late supper to top off my lone sandwich at El Patio, it was after midnight by then and sufficient time had passed for the radio news bureaus to hold telephone interviews with most everyone important enough to quote.

One after the other I tuned in all the local stations, then listened to what the nearest stations in Illinois had to say. The contrast was edifying. Our local stations quoted all the carefully correct statements made by our city and state officials, such as how shocked and grieved they were that a visiting dignitary should have been murdered this side of the river, and the people of Illinois could rest assured no stone would be left unturned in the effort to bring the assassin to speedy justice. At the same time the local announcers managed to imply the shooting must have been the work of gangsters from across the river. A European visitor listening to the broadcasts might have gotten the impression Walter Lancaster's was the first murder ever occurring in our state.

On the other hand the stations in Illinois delicately suggested Lancaster might still be alive had he stayed in the civilized state which elected him, where police were on duty to prevent the shooting of important citizens. Without being in the least discourteous, and in fact while professing the utmost confidence in the efficiency of our local police, they managed to get across the impression that anyone who entered our barbaric territory unarmed was virtually committing suicide. California and Florida are not the only two states where interstate competition flourishes.

Shortly after one, I grew tired of listening and was reaching for the radio switch just as another bulletin began. At the moment I was tuned to a local station, and my hand was already on the switch when the announcer's words froze it there.

'We have just received the first official statement from Inspector Warren Day of the Homicide Department,' the disk jockey who ran the Dawn Patrol said. 'Inspector Day has personally assumed charge of investigating the murder of Walter Lancaster, which occurred earlier this past evening. According to the inspector, a witness has been located who saw the assassin's face just as the shot was fired. The name of the witness is being withheld. Earlier reports indicated three persons saw the shooting: the doorman at the El Patio club, a taxi driver who was holding the door of his cab for Mr. Lancaster to enter when the shot was fired, and a customer who was just entering the club. The inspector states that none of these is the key witness, however, and that a fourth person who was standing in darkness at the corner of the building is the one who saw the killer's face. An arrest is expected within twenty-four hours.'

Switching off the radio, I phoned

Fausta at her apartment on the second floor of El Patio. The club closes at one, and she was already in bed, but not yet asleep.

'After I left, you actually wrote out and signed that statement about seeing the killer, didn't you?' I said.

'Of course,' she told me cheerfully. 'I could not see you go to jail, Manny.'

'For cripes' sake, Fausta. You know Warren Day didn't believe you, don't you?'

I could almost see her shrug. 'But he let you go free.'

'You hear the radio bulletin just now?'

'No.'

'Day released your statement — withholding your name, of course. But if they ever catch the killer and call you to testify in court, you'll be in a sweet spot. They put you in jail for perjury.'

Over the phone I could hear a kitten-like yawn. 'I will lie so nobody catches me, Manny. Do not worry so.'

'It isn't the lie that worries me so much,' I told her. 'It's Day making so much of it when he knows as well as I do it's a lie.

Knowing how the inspector's mind works, I smell the beginning of a killer trap with you as the bait.'

She was silent for a minute. 'You mean the killer might try to silence me because he thinks I could recognize his face?' Obviously this possibility had not previously occurred to her.

'What would you do if you had just committed a murder and then heard over the radio a witness could identify you?'

'Pooh!' she said. 'You're just trying to scare me. If the inspector withheld my name, how would the killer know who to look for?'

'He wouldn't, unless Day deliberately lets it leak out who his witness is. Does Mouldy still sleep downstairs off the kitchen?'

'Yes.'

'Tell him to keep his gun handy. I'll be around to see you sometime tomorrow.'

After I hung up and climbed into bed, it was another hour before I was able to get to sleep.

The next noon I had just awoken and was trying to summon enough energy to throw off the covers and sit erect, but not quite enough to get out of bed entirely.

The door buzzer accomplished what would have required at least another five minutes of mental struggle to accomplish, had it not sounded: it got me up.

Swinging my good left foot to the floor, I hopped to the bedroom door, shouted, 'It'll take me five minutes!' and hopped back to the edge of the bed again. I used the five minutes to strap on my leg, throw a handful of water in my face and dress to the extent of shoes, pants and a colored T-shirt.

When I finally opened the door, I said to the man I found standing in the hall, 'Sorry to keep you waiting. I sleep late on Tuesdays.' I also sleep late on Mondays, Wednesdays, Thursdays, Fridays, Saturdays and Sundays, but felt it unnecessary to mention this.

The man probably weighed two-thirty, and not an ounce of it was fat. He had a granite jaw and slow, sleepy eyes, and stood so straight he nearly leaned backward. The way he kept both hands in his pockets while he looked me over startled me for a moment, for my first thought was that he was training a concealed gun on me. But his pockets obviously contained nothing but hands. Apparently he was merely more comfortable that way.

He looked me over without saying anything for so long a time, I might have thought he was stunned with admiration had I been vain about my appearance. At length I asked, 'How did you ring the bell with your hands in your pockets? Use your nose?'

'You're Mr. Manville Moon?' he asked, ignoring my wit.

I said I was.

'I'm Laurence Davis.'

If his name was supposed to mean something to me, I missed the cue. A few more moments of silence ensued, and I began to suspect he was going to sleep. I said, 'I could sublease you that spot, but I would have to charge high rent to compensate for the inconvenience of having to use the back door. It would be hard to get in and out the front way with you standing there all the time.'

'You're a very funny man, Mr. Moon,'

he said, slowly moving toward me with his hands still in his pockets.

There was nothing belligerent in his movement, but there was an air of inexorability about it. He had decided he wanted to come in, and the fact that he had to walk over me unless I moved didn't deter him any. I stepped aside to avoid collision; he went past me with a kind of lazy ponderousness and took my personal easy chair. When he sat down, his hands came out of his pockets, and he took off his hat and held it in his lap.

Right behind him came a tall, narrow man who must have been standing in the hall to one side of the door all the time, for this was the first I knew of his presence. He was about thirty-five and had a doughy face and teeth so bucked he could not quite bring his lips together. His build was along the lines of Abe Lincoln's, and though he wore an obviously expensive blue serge, his gangling boniness made him look like a backwoods farmer dressed for church. By the bulge under his arm I judged he was not a farmer, however. I tagged him as a bodyguard, and when he closed the door, leaned his back against it and simply waited, I was sure of it. I waited too.

After a time the big man said, 'Apparently my name didn't ring a bell, Mr. Moon. I'm from across the river. Carson City, Illinois.'

It rang a bell now. The 'Laurence' had thrown me, for in the newspapers he was generally referred to less formally as Laurie Davis. The political boss of Illinois he was reputed to be, though he had never personally held a higher public office than state representative. According to rumor his business interests were so varied and his political influence so wide, he could have ruled Illinois as a benevolent dictator in the manner of Huey Long, had his ambitions run along those lines. However, he was supposed to be square, concerned more with the welfare of his party than with personal aggrandizement, as demonstrated by his remaining in the state legislature for twenty years when presumably he could have gone to Congress, or even become governor. Nevertheless he managed to collect enemies, and twice attempts had been made on his life. After the second attempt, about a year before, he had acquired his buck-toothed bodyguard.

Now that I had Laurie Davis placed, I also recognized the bodyguard. 'Farmer' Cole was an ex-FBI man who was supposed to be so tough that just his addition to the payroll decided the underworld group gunning for Davis to cancel their homicidal plans. The Farmer didn't *look* particularly tough. With his startling white teeth in constant evidence, your first impression was that his mouth was open in awe. But the expression on his face was completely blank, and his eyes were as flat as those of a dead fish.

Some people you instinctively like, and some you instinctively dislike. I experienced neither emotion about Farmer Cole, but I did feel a strange watchfulness, as though we were two suspicious dogs examining each other with raised hackles. He must have got the same feeling almost at the same instant I did, for a flicker of cold interest appeared in his flat eyes. Apparently to demonstrate his superior muscular co-ordination, his hand suddenly flashed from his pocket, a cigarette was in his mouth, and a lighted match was under it so rapidly the entire stunt was a blur of motion.

I turned back to his boss. 'I recognize you now, Mr. Davis. Out of your territory a little, aren't you?'

'All the way out of it. Sit down, Mr. Moon. I dislike gazing upward.'

Accepting his invitation to sit in my own apartment, I examined him interestedly. There was a curious air of latent power about him, in spite of his sleepy appearance. While his expression was placid, there was no humor in him, and it would not have strained the imagination to visualize him nodding casually to his bucktoothed bodyguard, then sleepily watching the Farmer kill a man.

He said, 'I came to you *because* I am out of my territory, Mr. Moon. I understand you were present when Walter Lancaster was killed last night.'

I admitted I had been. 'As a matter of fact I was a suspect for a few minutes,' I added calmly.

'So I understand. However, I am just as satisfied as the police that you had nothing to do with the killing. I'm not here to question you about last night, but to engage your services.'

I looked at him blankly.

'If this had happened in Illinois, I wouldn't have to bother with private investigators, Mr. Moon. But over here my influence is nil. Walt Lancaster was a protégé of mine, and I want his killer caught. But if the police catch him, I won't be able to control the situation. I want to get to the killer before they do.'

I said, 'I'm afraid I don't follow.'

His eyes drooped half-closed in his sleepy face. 'I'm simply taking insurance, Mr. Moon. As far as I know, Walt was an honest man and hadn't an enemy in the world. But people don't get murdered for nothing. If there was anything unsavory in Lancaster's background, it will come out in the open the minute the police crack the case. That might reflect both on me and the party. I want to know the killer's name and his motive before the police do, so I can plan some kind of action to counteract the unfavorable publicity, if any.'

I frowned at him. 'You mean have Farmer Cole here rub him out and save the state a trial?'

Slowly his lids raised until his eyes were wide open. 'I don't operate like a gangster, Mr. Moon,' he said in a soft voice. 'And I don't like the suggestion that I would.'

I don't scare easily, or at least I like to imagine I don't, but the big man's quiet air of invincibility gave me the willies. And as usual when anyone begins to give me a sense of inferiority, I had to convince myself I was twice as tough as he was.

I said, 'Quit making like Edwin G. Robinson and tell me what the hell you want.'

At a slight cough from the door, I turned my head to glance at the bucktoothed bodyguard. He simply looked at me, steadily and without expression. Had he advised me to show more respect for his boss, or made any remark at all, the effect would have been less deadly. But he simply looked, and I knew any time I wanted I could have any kind of fight I wanted: fists, guns or Bowie knives while we each held one end of a handkerchief in our teeth.

As though he hadn't heard my remark, Davis went on. 'I have no intention of doing anything to the killer. Not even turning him over to the police. I simply want to know what's behind the killing before the public does. At least twenty-four hours before. After that you may turn the killer over to the police or let him go, whichever suits your fancy.'

'You suspect what's behind it?' I asked.

He shrugged slowly. ''Suspect' is too strong a word. There is a bare possibility it may be something I wouldn't want made public unless I announced it myself. If Walt was involved in anything shady, I want to be the one to unearth it. Unless it comes from me, it will be hard to convince the public the party didn't know about it all along.'

'What is this thing you're afraid of?'

He shook his head. 'You'll have to work in the dark. I wouldn't even want it rumored unless I was sure. As a matter of fact I'm almost sure Walt Lancaster was scrupulously honest. But I don't run risks.'

I said, 'Let me get this straight. You simply want the killer's name and motive? You don't want him delivered to you?'

Again he shook his head. 'I don't even care to know where he is. I'm not after revenge, but simply taking a political precaution.'

Somewhere I sensed more than just that. I had an idea he had given me all the information he intended to, which amounted to exactly nothing, but I tried once more. 'Before you hired Farmer Cole to guard your body, a couple of people took pot shots at you, as I remember. Any chance Lancaster's killer might be one of those people?'

'It's a possibility,' he admitted without enthusiasm.

'Ever figure out who those people were?'

He shook his head.

'Ever *suspect* who they were?'

He regarded me from beneath sleepy lids. 'You're a persistent questioner, Mr. Moon. No evidence was ever turned up concerning the two attempts on my life. However, at the time I was bringing my influence to bear on cleaning up certain illegal rackets operating in my county. I managed to make it so uncomfortable for the racketeers involved, they finally moved to an adjacent county, where they've been operating ever since. If my plans work out, eventually I'll run them right across the river to bother you people.'

'That will be nice for us,' I said. 'Would you know the names of any of these racketeers?'

'The supposed ringleader is mentioned in the papers occasionally. Nothing has ever been proved.'

I admired his caution. He was not going to defame anyone's character in front of witnesses unless he had documentary proof the guy had no character. But I am not so sensitive about slandering known hoods.

'Barney Seldon is sometimes mentioned in the papers,' I said.

'Yes. I've read about him.'

'Barney Seldon was also at El Patio last night. I saw the cops put the collar on him for later questioning.'

'Yes, I know. He was released after questioning, which means he at least satisfied the police he had nothing to do with Walt's death.' He changed the subject by saying, 'I'm willing to pay two thousand dollars plus expenses. One thousand now and one thousand if you deliver me the information at least twenty-four hours before it becomes public.'

'It's a deal,' I said quickly, before he could change his mind. Then I said, 'You mentioned you're just as satisfied as the police that I didn't shoot your protégé, but you don't impress me as the type of person who makes snap judgments. What convinced you?'

'I talked to the eyewitness who saw the killer,' he said calmly.

I felt the hair rise along the back of my neck. In a cautious voice I asked, 'Who was that?'

For the first time he almost smiled. 'You know as well as I, Mr. Moon. And you don't have to fear my making it public so the killer will know whom to eliminate. I've been a regular customer of

El Patio for years and feel as friendly toward Miss Moreni as you do. Incidentally, it was Fausta who recommended you to me.'

I closed my eyes for a minute, wondering how many other people Fausta had told her story to in an effort to protect me, for knowing how Fausta's mind worked, it was obvious to me she had deliberately placed me above suspicion in Laurie Davis's eyes in order to make me safe from possible vengeance. At least she was consistent in her perjury, but if she continued repeating herself often enough, there was a fair chance the so-called key witness's identity would get back to the killer.

I decided I had better speak firmly to Fausta.

4

I don't think I have ever encountered a client as unwilling to impart information as Laurie Davis. The worst of it was, I had a feeling he could tell me exactly what he wanted me to look for, but preferred that I start the investigation cold without benefit of whatever theory he himself had. He reminded me of the kind of guy who refuses to tell his symptoms to the doctor because he wants the doctor to earn his money without help. Only the size of his fee prevented me from tossing his check back at him and advising him to solve his protégé's murder himself. But two thousand dollars can compensate for a lot of temperament in a client.

About all I got from Davis was a little background material on Walter Lancaster, and even that contained nothing I could not have dug from a newspaper morgue had I wanted to take the time.

Prior to entering politics Lancaster had

been legal advisor and vice president of the Illinois Telegraph Company at a salary of fifty thousand dollars a year. He had served no political apprenticeship, jumping from business into a key political position much in the manner of Wendell Willkie. He left a widow, a college-age son and an estate Laurie Davis estimated might run into two million dollars. Most of this, Davis believed, was in corporate stocks, as Walter Lancaster had been on the board of directors of four small corporations in addition to his primary job with the Illinois Telegraph Company, and presumably he would not have been elected to these boards unless he had substantial investments in the companies.

The only point on which Davis seemed willing to impart detailed information was the lieutenant governor's business connections. He told me the four corporations on whose boards Lancaster had served were Rockaway Distributors (a wholesale magazine and news company), Ilco Utilities, Eastern Plow Manufacturers, Inc. and the Palmer Tools Company. All were Illinois firms.

Deciding I could get more information than my client had to offer from almost anyone I asked, including the shoeshine boy on the corner, I took Davis's private phone number in Carson City and told him I would report the minute I had anything definite. After he and his gangling bodyguard departed, I shaved, dressed and cooked myself a combination breakfast and lunch, it then being nearly one p.m.

Instead of breaking my back going over ground already covered by the police, I decided the best place to start my investigation was to learn what they knew. And the best source for that was Warren Day. While it would be padding the truth to say I ever look forward with pleasure to an interview with the inspector, I do derive a certain stimulation from our encounters. For eight years Inspector Warren Day and I have maintained a cooperative agreement: I get in his hair and he gets in mine. A casual observer would think he hated my guts, which he probably does part of the time, but on the few occasions other division heads of the local police department have started pushing me around, Day has shooed them off like a mother hen protecting her young. I have never quite decided whether this phenomenon is due to some spark of affection for me he conceals under his crusty exterior, or whether he simply has me marked off for pushing around by the chief of Homicide only, and resents others poaching on his private game.

I found my scrawny friend in his office hunched over a sheaf of written reports. When I entered, he raised his skinny bald head to peer at me over his glasses and snarled, 'Can't you knock, Moon?'

I had anticipated finding him in a sour mood, for I guessed from his pixie attitude the previous night he did not realize what was in store for him in investigating Lancaster's murder. But by now he would have received phone calls from the commissioner, the mayor, the governor, a couple of congressmen and a dozen other assorted public figures, all urging him to catch the assassin post-haste. He was used to pressure and usually could shrug it off, but a mere police inspector can't shrug off that kind of pressure.

Had I not been convinced he was playing some kind of dangerous game with Fausta, I would have felt a little sorry for him, for since Day had become chief of Homicide, no one approaching Lancaster's importance had been murdered in the city, and the amount of pressure he was already beginning to feel certainly must have appalled him.

But thinking of the radio release he had made caused me to snarl back at him, 'What are you trying to pull on Fausta Moreni?'

The inspector only growled and returned to his reports. Sinking into a chair, I regained his attention by pinching a cigar from his desk humidor.

'You've got two cigars sticking out of your breast pocket!' he snapped.

'Stolen apples taste better.' Biting off the end of the cigar, I unsuccessfully felt in my pockets. 'Got a match?'

All that got me was a glare. Shrugging, I decided to chew instead of smoke. 'I won't take much of your time,' I said. 'I only came in for two things. The first I already asked you.'

'You mean about Miss Moreni? I don't know what you're talking about.'

'Don't get coy with me, Inspector. We've known each other too long. You know as well as I do that statement of Fausta's is meaningless. Why play it up?'

He gave me a smile like a cat with feathers in its whiskers. 'When a witness signs a statement, Moon, I have every right to assume it's the truth. Of course she can repudiate it, but in that case I'd have to accept Robert Caxton's statement and take you into custody.'

I said disgustedly, 'You don't believe either statement. You're using Fausta to try to smoke out the killer. I suppose your next move will be to let the eyewitness's identity leak.'

Day looked wounded. 'We're not that crude, Moon. You think we'd deliberately set up a young woman as a target?'

'Yes.'

He examined me in silence for a minute. 'It's none of your business,' he said finally, 'but just to relieve your mind, I'll tell you what we're doing. I have tails on that taxi driver and doorman.'

I looked at him blankly. 'For what?'

'Put yourself in the killer's place,' he said irritably. 'You read in the paper a witness has seen your face. The name isn't given, but the names of three other witnesses who *didn't* see your face are. Possibly these witnesses, or at least one of them, knows who the fourth witness is. Is it worth the risk of approaching them one at a time in an attempt to learn the fourth witness's identity?'

I thought of something. 'Have you got a tail on me too?' I demanded.

Day shook his head. 'If the killer bites at all, we figure he would steer away from a private detective except as a last resort. And even if he did approach you, we assume you'd have sense enough to sit on him and give us a buzz.'

I thought of something else. 'The other witnesses actually do know who the fourth is, because we were all present when Fausta made that silly statement. Suppose the killer does contact one of them, gets the information he wants, and your man loses him?'

Warren Day frowned, opened his mouth and closed it again. Finally he rumbled, 'We don't make mistakes like that.' I emitted a polite laugh. 'If we figure Miss Moreni is in any danger, we'll take her into protective custody,' he snapped.

'Swell,' I said bitterly. 'Put her in jail.'

'Better than being dead,' he offered in a reasonable tone. 'Get on with the second thing you want. I'm pretty busy.'

'I want to help you,' I told him. 'As a patriotic citizen, I feel it my duty to do something about this blot on our city's honor.'

Day regarded me suspiciously. 'Do you know something you didn't tell last night?'

'Not yet,' I admitted. 'I plan to crack the case as soon as you tell me what you've got so far.'

He glared at me with sudden indignation. 'You're on the case? It's not enough I got the district attorney, two governors and every newspaper in the country on my back. Now you want to breathe down my neck. Go away.'

He dropped his eyes back to the reports on his desk. I sat quietly chewing my filched cigar. Finally he looked up again. 'Who's your client?' he asked me.

'The governor of Illinois.'

He snorted. Searching his ashtray, he found a long cigar butt, blew the ashes from it and stuck it in his mouth. I waited for him to produce a match, but he preferred merely to chew also.

'Laurie Davis was seen in town this morning,' he said, eying me expectantly.

'He was?'

'Is he your client?' he demanded.

'My client wants to remain incognito.'

He started to glare, but let it deteriorate into what was supposed to be an ingratiating smile.

I knew what was going through his mind. If my client actually was Laurie Davis, he could hardly afford to be uncooperative, for even the governor might listen attentively if the political boss of a neighboring state decided to make a complaint. And with pressure on the department already tremendous, Day had no desire to make it any worse.

Apparently the inspector decided to take no chances, and the decision brought about one of his abrupt changes in manner which never fail to fascinate me. All at once he was full of wheedling friendliness. 'We're always willing to cooperate with you private fellows when you cooperate with us, Manny. I'll be glad to give you the little bit we got, if you'll promise to turn in everything you find out the minute you find it — not a week or two later, as you sometimes do.'

'Let's make a deal,' I said.

Immediately he was suspicious again. 'What kind of deal?'

'I'll hold nothing back at all from you, if you'll promise the same treatment.'

'Sure, Manny,' he said, relieved and a little surprised, for he seemed to hold the erroneous impression that he generally came out second when we horse traded.

'There's one qualification,' I said. 'I want you to agree that regardless of which one of us breaks the case, we keep the arrest secret for twenty-four hours.'

Straightening in his chair, he looked at

me with amazement. 'Why should I agree to a silly thing like that?'

'There's a political reason,' I said casually.

Day opened his mouth, closed it again and glared at me speechlessly. The two things in the world he understands not at all are women and politics, and it is a toss-up as to which frightens him more.

'No politician is going to tell me how to run Homicide,' he declared unconvincingly.

'None want to,' I assured him. 'You'll have your killer, and no one will interfere with the legal prosecution. All I'm asking is he be held as a material witness or some such thing for twenty-four hours. Assuming we ever catch him, that is. If he can't, we'll have to work independently, because I'm committed to work on that basis only.'

'Why?'

'Because I am. Do we cooperate, or do I tell Laurie Davis I'm on my own?'

I let the name slip deliberately, and watched Day's reaction to the confirmation that my client was who he suspected.

'For an old friend like you I think we can arrange that,' he said in a choked voice.

So our agreement was made, and the inspector proceeded to bring me up to date.

As I had surmised from the double wound, the bullet which killed Lancaster had passed entirely through his body. The spent slug, too badly battered from striking a rib on the way out to make comparison tests possible in the event the murder weapon was ever found, was located lying on the gravel drive only a few feet from the body. Since no ejected casing was found, it was assumed the weapon had been a revolver rather than an automatic.

A thin coating of dried leaves from the previous fall had been spread over the close-cropped grass as fertilizer by El Patio's gardener, and the resulting spongy turf left no footprints. However, a muzzle flash had singed a bush at the edge of the drive, so it had been possible to determine where the killer had been standing.

At this point I interrupted. 'Then my story is verified without Fausta's statement. If she repudiates it, that taxi driver's imaginings still don't mean anything.'

Racketeer Barney Seldon had been held for questioning as a matter of routine, the inspector went on calmly, but since he was still seated at his table in the midst of over a hundred other diners when the shot was fired, he was not even booked. It developed that he was a habitué of El Patio, dining there several nights a week, so there was nothing unusual about his being present at the time of the murder. Except for his reputation for violence, the police had no reason to connect him with the affair.

'Right after you left I sent Hannegan over to Carson City to break the news to Lancaster's wife,' Day went on. 'A lousy job, but somebody always has to do it. He found out from Mrs. Lancaster the dead man's purpose in being this side of the river was a business meeting with some investment brokers, and she had expected him home last night. He also found out practically everybody knew Lancaster would be at El Patio last night. During a luncheon speech in Carson City a few days back he made a humorous reference to a charge by a political rival that he was in the pay of a restaurant-owners' lobby which was trying to get the state sanitary code relaxed. He said his influence among restaurateurs was so great that when he phoned El Patio a week in advance for a seven-thirty dinner reservation for last night, he only had to argue about twenty minutes in order to get himself fitted in an hour later than he wanted. The speech was reprinted in the Carson City *Herald*, so anyone who can read could have known he would be coming out of El Patio about nine thirty.'

'Who were the investment brokers he met with?' I asked.

'Jones and Knight Investment Company on Broadway. I sent a man over this morning and he talked to one of the partners. Guy named Harlan Jones. According to him, Lancaster left the brokerage office alone at five p.m. Offhand this looks to me like a political assassination by some fanatic.'

I said, 'Remember a while back when a couple of pot shots were taken at Laurie Davis?'

He nodded. 'Before he hired that ex-FBI fellow as a bodyguard.'

'There's a probability Barney Seldon was behind those attempts.'

Day peered at me over his glasses. 'How would you know a thing like that?'

'I don't,' I told him. 'It's only a guess. But it's a guess founded on pretty sound reasoning. Did you know Laurie Davis ran Seldon's rackets out of his county?'

'No. I don't pay much attention to Illinois crime. I've got enough troubles of my own.'

'Well, he did,' I said. 'And if you read the papers, you'd know Davis literally hand-picked Walter Lancaster for lieutenant governor. Maybe Barney was striking back at Davis by having his protégé knocked off.'

'A little roundabout for a hood like Seldon,' Day said dubiously. 'He'd be more likely to have Davis himself bumped. Besides, he has a perfect alibi.'

'So what? He wouldn't do his own gun

work. He probably has a dozen gunnies he could call on.'

The inspector gave his head a shake of disagreement. 'We'll watch for him to come across the river again and go over him some more, but I can't see Barney Seldon behind this. If he ordered it, he wouldn't go out of his way to be on the spot. He'd have a perfect alibi a hundred miles from the murder.'

'Maybe,' I suggested, 'that's exactly what he figured the police would think.'

5

A slightly inebriated associate professor of philosophy I met in a barroom one night explained to me the difference between deductive and inductive reasoning. The former is the method employed by that galaxy of fiction sleuths who make their livings solving crimes without ever getting out of their chairs. When fictional homicide chiefs humbly call on a fictional deductive reasoner to lay before him problems they are unable to solve themselves, he leans back, closes his eyes and thinks. And simply by putting in logical order the information the police already have, he pops up with an answer.

The French philosopher Descartes is an example of pure deductive reasoning, the philosophy professor told me in exchange for buying him a boilermaker; and when I only looked at him blankly, he came down to my level by putting C. Auguste Dupin and Sherlock Holmes in the same category.

The inductive reasoner is not satisfied with merely known facts, he further instructed me. He attempts to dig up all *possible* facts related to the problem, and when he has them all, he expects certain conclusions to appear as self-evident without having to link his facts together into a logical chain. This, the professor expounded, is both the method of modern science and the method of modern criminology.

I was pleasantly surprised to discover I was so modern, for I was an inductive rather than deductive reasoner even before I met the philosophy professor. No doubt I could use the deductive method if some humble homicide chief would call to feed me facts, but the only homicide chief I know is Warren Day; and while he sometimes calls at my flat, usually it is because he is thirsty. Consequently, I depend more on my car and my feet than I do on cold logic. My routine is simple in a case like Walter Lancaster's. I simply interview everybody I can think of who might know something about him.

My first move was to see the murdered

man's family in Carson City, which in spite of being only a few miles distant, took most of the afternoon by the time I had fought bridge traffic both coming and going. I did not anticipate the visit would be very fruitful, since Hannegan had already interviewed the widow, and the stocky lieutenant rarely misses a bet. It was just as fruitful as I anticipated.

The widow was a rather plain woman of middle age, dry-eyed and controlled, but obviously grief-stricken. The son, a redheaded youngster named Rodney, impressed me as being more angry than sad. He had driven home from the University of Illinois, where he was a sophomore, the moment he heard the news, and was raring to tear somebody apart for shooting his dad.

From neither of them did I learn anything which seemed to me at the time to possess value. I did get verification of Laurie Davis's statement about Lancaster having been a director of four corporations aside from Illinois Telegraph before he resigned all directorships to run for lieutenant governor. But neither Mrs. Lancaster nor Rodney had more than the vaguest understanding of his business affairs.

From the widow I also learned Lancaster had seemed rather upset his last few days, and she got the impression his pending meeting with the Jones and Knight Company was what bothered him. Since he never discussed business matters at home, she had no idea what the meeting was about, but she volunteered the information that one of the partners was an old friend of Lancaster's. Her husband and Willard Knight had attended the University of Illinois together, she said, and though in recent years they had only rare contact, on the infrequent occasions her husband mentioned Knight's name, he always referred to him as though he were a close friend. Actually the two men had not been close at all since college days, she added. As a matter of fact they saw each other so rarely, she had never met Knight herself. She had a vague recollection of her husband mentioning only a week or two back that he had encountered Willard Knight somewhere by accident and the two had lunch together.

Aside from that, the trip was a waste of time. Neither could suggest any reason whatever why anyone would want to kill Lancaster. And to make the afternoon a complete fiasco, I had to let the last person in the world to whom I cared to be indebted save me from being run over.

The Lancaster home was right on Carson City's main street, which is also part of a through highway. I had parked across the road, and I started back across to my car just as a couple of kids in a convertible roared through town at what must have been ninety miles an hour.

I always look before crossing streets, just as I was taught in kindergarten, checking first to the left and then to the right. The highway was clear when I glanced left, but in the half-second it took me to glance right and take one step into the road, the convertible lifted out of a dip a hundred yards away and bore down at me with its horn screaming.

My reactions are fast, but a false leg is unpredictable. My nerves activated the proper muscles in plenty of time to get me out of the way, but the leg picked that moment to buckle. Slipping to the knee of my good leg, I tried to scramble to the curb on all fours, realized I wasn't going to make it, then suddenly was jerked clear by a pair of hands which gripped both biceps and nearly tore my arms loose from my shoulders.

Since I couldn't stand until my leg was refastened, I didn't bother to look at my rescuer until I had rolled up my pants leg, readjusted the straps above and below my knee, rolled down the pants leg again and dusted myself off. Then I climbed to my feet and looked into the bucktoothed face of Farmer Cole.

'Where'd you come from?' I asked sourly, then added reluctantly, 'Thanks.'

'I live in this town,' he said. 'You're welcome.'

'Oh. Well, thanks again.' I tried to make this one more enthusiastic, but it still came out sour. Even after the guy had saved my life, I couldn't shake the feeling of tense watchfulness his nearness induced in me.

I turned to try the crossing again.

'Want me to help you across?' the Farmer asked.

Slowly I turned to look at him. 'That crack makes us even, Farmer. You saved my life; now I'm saving yours by ignoring the crack.'

He grinned at me, a grin as sardonic as Bugs Bunny's. With dignity I crossed to my car, first looking carefully both ways, climbed under the wheel and glanced back to where he had been standing.

He had disappeared.

Since the only lead I had picked up in Carson City was the widow's vague idea that Lancaster had been worried over his impending conference with the Jones and Knight Investment Company, I decided to take a chance on finding someone still at the company office, even though it was just five o'clock when I drove off the bridge on my own side of the river. Stopping at the first tavern I saw for a glance in the phone book, I discovered the office was only a few blocks up Broadway, just south of the Federal Reserve Building. I made it by ten after five and found a parking place right in front of the entrance.

According to the building directory, the

Jones and Knight Investment Company was on the fourth floor. A woman took me up in an elevator, informing me as I got off that the elevators stopped running at six.

Though the office building in which it was housed was old and beginning to look run-down in a genteel sort of way, the office of Jones and Knight had an air of prosperity about it. Thick carpeting covered the floor of the reception room, the furniture was solidly expensive, and Venetian blinds hung at the windows.

A middle-aged woman wearing horn-rimmed glasses sat at a desk in the reception room. Apparently I would have missed her had I been five minutes later, for she was just powdering her nose in preparation to go home.

'Mr. Jones or Mr. Knight in?' I asked.

'No, sir,' she said politely. 'We close at five. Did you have an appointment?'

I shook my head. 'I'm a private investigator inquiring into the Lancaster killing.' I let her look at my license and took a soft leather chair while she was examining it.

She looked it over so long I got the impression she was using it as an excuse to gather herself together after the shock of my announcement. Her reaction intrigued me. 'My name is Matilda Graves, Mr. Moon,' she said finally. 'I'm secretary and bookkeeper of the firm. You know, of course, the police have already been here.'

'Yes, but something new has come up since their visit. Are you the only employee aside from the partners, Miss Graves?'

She nodded, not quite seeming to trust her voice.

'Are you sufficiently in Jones's and Knight's confidence to know what Mr. Lancaster's meeting with them was about yesterday?'

Quickly she shook her head. 'Mr. Lancaster wasn't an account of ours, Mr. Moon. He was merely an old friend of Mr. Knight's. Naturally I would have known, or at least been able to guess, what his business with Mr. Knight was had Mr. Lancaster been one of our accounts. It would be hard for an investment company bookkeeper not to know the business affairs of most of the company's clients. But this was a personal business matter between Mr. Lancaster and Mr. Knight.'

'How do you know it was a personal *business* matter if you don't know what it was? Couldn't it have been a personal social matter?'

I asked the question in an easy tone, with no intention of upsetting her, but she surprised me by turning dead white. 'The police never questioned me at all,' she said in a faint voice. 'I've been driving myself crazy trying to decide whether or not I ought to contact them. But if I caused Mr. Knight trouble and there was nothing to it, I might lose my job. Anyway — '

'What about Mr. Knight?' I prompted.

'I thought about talking it over with Mr. Jones and asking his advice, but he doesn't know anything about it, and that would put him in the same position I'm in — making trouble for Mr. Knight, I mean. And after all, they're partners, so you see it would be uncomfortable for him. He's such a nice man. Mr. Jones, I mean, not Mr. Knight.' She added hurriedly, 'Not that Mr. Knight isn't nice too, but I mean — '

I said, 'Just a minute, Miss Graves. Take a deep breath and start at the beginning.'

It took her a long time and I had to interrupt with questions about every third sentence, but I finally pieced together what was bothering her. She said Walter Lancaster had met with Knight in the latter's office at about three p.m., and the two had argued for two hours. Jones had been using a dictaphone in his own office, which was right next to Knight's, and had not been present at the conference.

I stopped her long enough to ask if she had gotten the impression Jones was deliberately excluded from the conference, or simply had not bothered to attend.

'Why neither, I think,' she said. 'Since it wasn't a company matter, but a personal thing between Mr. Lancaster and Mr. Knight, I suppose Mr. Jones had no reason to sit in. He did go in for a minute once, when Mr. Knight started shouting, I guess to calm him down. But he came right out again and went back to his own office. Mr. Knight didn't shout any more, but he had left the key open on his call box, and I heard everything he and Mr. Lancaster said.'

It developed there had been quite an argument. Miss Graves did not catch it all (she explained her mind was too occupied with her own duties to listen closely, though I suspect the real reason she missed portions of the argument was that it is difficult to hear over an inter-office communication system unless the speaker speaks directly into the box), but she gathered the reason for Walter Lancaster's visit was to learn if his old school chum had actually invested in a stock he had discussed with Lancaster some weeks previously.

Apparently Knight had, for when the lieutenant governor announced he had unearthed some kind of irregularity in the corporation which issued the stock, and intended to make it public the next day, Knight blew up. He insisted Lancaster had induced him to buy the stock, an accusation Lancaster flatly denied, declaring that while he had no intimation at the time of their discussion that the corporation was shaky, Knight knew very well he never gave market advice to anyone, and certainly he would not have presumed to give it to a professional investment broker.

Grudgingly Knight admitted that while Lancaster might not have recommended the investment, he had given the impression he considered it a sound one, and the least he could do was hold off his announcement twenty-four hours so that both of them could unload.

Lancaster declared he would not allow the public to be cheated any more than it already had been. He said that while no one but himself as yet knew of the stock's false value, a rumor about a possible boom in its value (which rumor apparently had induced Knight to invest) had the other major stockholders watching it closely. A sudden dumping by two of the large stockholders would cause others to dump too, he said, and result in the usual situation of letting small stockholders take the rap while those who could best afford the loss scurried to safety. Patiently he explained a fact which must have been obvious to Knight as an investment broker: that saving themselves were possible only by sticking someone else. He held the revolutionary theory that it was as dishonest for a stockholder to dump stock he knew was worthless as it was for a corporation to issue such stock. In both cases, he pointed out, you are offering the public an investment you know may ruin the investors; and the fact that it was not only legal, but was not even regarded as unethical in market circles, did not alter his opinion that morally it was outright fraud.

He felt it a moral duty for the current stockholders to bear the loss, Lancaster concluded. He himself had no intention of unloading his own stock, even though it meant the immediate loss of three-fourths of his fortune.

I found myself mentally giving Lancaster points for unselfishness, but at the same time it occurred to me that if Laurie

Davis's estimate of his protégé's worth was accurate, a seventy-five percent loss would still leave him a rich man. Knight, on the other hand, probably lacked the cushion of two million dollars to fall back on.

Matilda Graves verified my thought when she went on to say that Knight had angrily assured Lancaster he had no intention of being ruined by the latter's misguided sense of honesty, and he would 'find a way' to prevent the announcement being made. At that point the lieutenant governor had walked out of the office and slammed the door.

'What was Jones's reaction to all this?' I asked curiously.

'Oh, he didn't know it,' the woman said. 'You see, he left shortly after four, while they were still arguing. At five he phoned from home and asked if Mr. Knight was still tied up in conference. I told him Mr. Lancaster had just left, but Mr. Knight was still here. He said to tell Mr. Knight he was flying to Kansas City at six and would be back in the morning. I didn't tell him anything about the argument.'

'And you haven't mentioned it since?'

'No. I hated to upset Mr. Jones. He's such a nice man. You see, when the police talked to Mr. Jones this morning, he told them Mr. Lancaster had left the office alone at five and he didn't know where he went from here. I guess they got the impression Mr. Jones had seen him leave, whereas actually he was merely repeating what I told him over the phone. And they never asked me anything.'

'Didn't the police talk to Knight also?'

She shook her head. 'Mr. Knight didn't come in today. When he failed to arrive this morning, Mr. Jones had me phone his home and Mrs. Knight said he was out of town visiting a customer.'

'Where?' I asked.

'She didn't say.' Her lips trembled a trifle and she blurted out, 'I think he's hiding!'

'Hiding? Why? Even if he killed Lancaster, presumably he would figure no one had reason to suspect him. Unless you told him the key to his call box was open.'

'I did,' she said.

'What?'

'I did tell him. Right after Mr. Lancaster left, Mr. Knight called me over the intercom. He said, 'My key seems to be open, Miss Graves. Has it been all along?' I said, 'Yes, sir.' He growled, 'Hope you got an earful,' and shut it off.'

'Sounds like a pleasant guy to work for,' I said. 'Do you have access to all company records?'

She nodded. 'I keep the books.'

'Think you could figure out what company Lancaster was talking about to Knight?'

She pursed her lips dubiously. 'I doubt that it would appear in our records. Both partners handle their own personal financial transactions, so they don't run through our books. I doubt that this office even has a record of the stock Mr. Knight owns. He would have that at home.'

'Look anyway, will you, and I'll phone you tomorrow. I can narrow the search somewhat for you, because Lancaster held stock in only five corporations: Illinois Telegraph, Rockaway Distributors, Ilco Utilities, Eastern Plow, and Palmer Tools.'

'I'll do my best,' she promised.

One good turn deserves another, and since she was willing to go to some trouble for me, I felt the least I could do in return was try to ease her worry over possessing knowledge she felt the police should have.

Rising, I said, 'Thanks very much for your information, Miss Graves. And don't fret about the police any more. I'm working with them, and I'll pass everything along.'

She seemed as pathetically grateful as a death-row prisoner who unexpectedly receives a pardon.

6

My next stop was the scene of the crime. By arriving at El Patio so early, I missed the pleasure of having my back bruised by Mouldy Greene's greeting, as he did not assume his post inside the entrance until seven.

I found Fausta in the office beyond the dining room, which at the moment was only half-full, but by seven would be crammed to the walls with people eager to pay El Patio's outrageous prices. She was seated at the desk, which always looked too large for her, frowning at a newly printed menu. The previous evening, Lancaster's murder and the attendant excitement had dampened Fausta's normal exuberance, but tonight she was back in usual form.

'Manny!' she cried, running around the desk, flinging herself into my arms, and planting an impassioned kiss on my chin.

After this spontaneous display of affection, she pushed me away just as though I had been the aggressor, narrowed her eyes at me, and lightly slapped my face. 'You rat,' she said. 'Where have you been all day?'

'Did you expect me earlier?' I asked. 'You know what a social whirl I whirl in. Other women expect some of my time.'

'Pooh!' she said. 'No woman but me would want a man of such ugliness.' Jumping up to seat herself on the desktop, she folded her arms and regarded me like a traffic-court judge. 'I can give you only a few minutes. You are not the only one chased by the opposite sex. I expect a man who loves me at any moment.'

'Well, if you've got a date, I'll come back later.'

But she was past me with her back to the door before I could even turn around. 'Not so fast, my love. What do you want? You never come just to see me anymore. You are here on business.'

'Partly,' I admitted. 'But mainly to tell you to stop broadcasting the lie that you were an eyewitness to the murder.'

She looked puzzled. 'Broadcasting?'

'You told Laurie Davis. I appreciate

your motive was to make sure he didn't suspect me, but you've got to cut it out. I don't want to be picking bullets out of your lovely skin.'

Fausta looked interested. 'You are worried about me, Manny?'

'Enough to straighten you out for good if I hear of you telling anyone else,' I said grimly. 'You so much as mention you're Day's key witness again, and I'll arrange to have the inspector stick you in protective custody. You want to sit in jail till we catch this killer?'

'You would not be so mean. And if you were, I would not tell you what I kept back from Inspector Day last night.'

'You kept something back?' I asked cautiously.

'Yes. You may have it for taking me out just once.'

I laughed. 'You don't have to blackmail me, Fausta. You know I'd rather take you out than do anything.' I would too, but it only starts me wondering whether it really matters which partner has the money, and by the time I decide it does and back off, the pain is likely to be as acute as that of a man suddenly pulled off the dope habit.

Fausta said, 'Will you take me out tomorrow night?'

'The next night.'

'Tomorrow,' she said firmly. 'Nine o'clock. Or I phone Inspector Day and tell him what I forgot.'

I gave up, as I always do. 'All right. Nine o'clock. Now give.'

The bargaining expression disappeared and she smiled. 'Barney Seldon was here last night.'

I said, 'Both the inspector and I already know that.'

'Be silent until I finish. He entered just after Mr. Lancaster and took a table facing his. The reason I noticed is because Barney has been paying me attention. In fact he is the man I am awaiting now.' She paused to smile expectantly.

'I'm insanely jealous,' I growled. 'Get on with it.'

'All during the meal Barney watched Mr. Lancaster. I noticed because Barney is such a handsome man, and I like to look at him. He is not ugly like you, and also he loves me more than you do.' She looked at me inquiringly.

'No doubt.'

She frowned. 'I also love him,' she said recklessly.

'Sure. That's why you're ratting on him. Listen, I love you madly, and I'll kill Barney Seldon with my bare hands if he so much as caresses your fingers. Now get on with it.'

'You do not mean it,' she said sulkily. 'Mr. Lancaster finished his dinner before Barney, and left while Barney waited for dessert. His dessert was delivered just as the shot came from out front.'

'Wait a minute,' I said. 'You told me you had just stepped outside from the ballroom's side door when the gun went off. How'd you manage to be two places at once?'

Without pause she said glibly, 'I watched Barney up to the moment I entered the ballroom. His waiter told me what happened afterward.'

'All right,' I conceded. 'Go on.'

'Barney was not at the table when his dessert was delivered.'

For a long time I looked at her. 'Where

was he?' I asked finally.

She shrugged. 'There is a cigarette machine by the side door. A minute or two after the shot, Barney returned from that direction with a package of cigarettes in his hand.'

'Could be coincidence,' I said slowly.

'Maybe. But there is also a cigarette machine in the cocktail lounge, which was much nearer Barney's table. Also he did not open the pack, but after his dessert took a cigarette from his case, which was full.'

'So he could have stepped out the dining room's side door, ducked across the drive in the dark, plugged Lancaster, and got back in again in a matter of seconds,' I said thoughtfully. 'I suppose the cops searched him though.'

'Perhaps he threw away the gun.'

'It wasn't found. Besides, I heard the killer, or at least somebody, run off after the shot and scoot away in a car. Barney isn't accustomed to doing his own killing anyway. If he's our lad, I like it better that he used the side door to signal a confederate Lancaster was leaving by the front.'

'Figure it any way you want,' Fausta

said. 'Just so you do not forget to come for me at nine tomorrow night.'

'You say you expect Seldon again tonight?' I asked.

'I expect him every night. Twenty miles he drives just to see me.'

'Maybe it's the food,' I suggested. 'There's something I don't understand. What made you stand around watching Seldon so closely?'

'I told you he is a handsome man.'

'Nuts,' I said. 'You're holding something back. If Barney is as hot after you as you say, he'd have had his eye on you too. And if he thought you had nothing better to do than stand around looking at him, he'd have had you over at his table.'

She frowned at me. 'I am a very reserved woman. I do not wish Barney to know how much I admire him, so I watched him from behind one of the potted palms.'

Before I could express my opinion of this obviously barefaced lie, a knock sounded at the door, then it immediately swung open. Mouldy Greene entered.

I said, 'Hello, Mouldy,' then quickly

side-stepped when his face beamed with friendliness and he raised a hand the size of a pancake.

'Hi yuh, Sarge?' he inquired, merely waving the hand instead of fracturing my spine with it. Then he scowled at Fausta. 'Romeo Seldon just come in and took his usual table. He asked for you, but I told him you had mumps.'

Fausta said quickly, 'I'll talk to you about it later, Mouldy,' and started to shoo him out of the office.

'Wait a minute,' I said, suddenly getting an idea. 'What's your opinion of Barney Seldon, Mouldy?'

'Same as Fausta's. He's a jerk. She tell you about last night?'

'Yeah. How come you were watching him so closely?'

''Cause he's a jerk, see. Sometimes he don't want to take my word for it Fausta's busy, and starts back for the office on his own. Then I got to put my arm on him so he don't bother her.'

Fausta stamped her foot. 'You lie, Mouldy Greene! Barney Seldon is a big romance in my life. I go now to supervise his dinner with my own loving hands.' And she went out, slamming the office door behind her.

Mouldy stared at the closed door in astonishment. 'Dames!' he commented. 'She tells me to keep the jerk off her neck, now all of a sudden she's nuts about the guy.'

'You told Fausta about Seldon's peculiar actions last night, eh?' I asked.

'Sure. And she said to clam up about it. When the cops asked questions, I just pretended to be stupid.'

'That must have required wonderful acting. How about introducing me to Barney Seldon?'

'Sure, Sarge. If you think you can stand him.'

My meeting with Barney Seldon was not exactly a success, primarily because I don't know how to be subtle with hoods. I can't resist the impulse to push them around, even when they're supposed to be big shots, for I don't recognize degrees of importance in hoods. As I look at it, living in a mansion and riding in a Cadillac doesn't give a hood any more social status than the punks you see in a morning police showup. No doubt this is a laudable sentiment, but it tends to get me in trouble.

Barney Seldon was in his early thirties and looked like a movie idol. He had a wide, pale face with features like a Trojan's and a nicely cleft chin. His shoulders didn't require padding to make his dinner jacket look like it was supposed to look, and his waist would have suited a girl.

Apparently he had not yet ordered dinner, for he was sipping a cocktail when we went over to his table. Fausta was not in sight, presumably being in the kitchen preparing food for Barney with her own loving hands, or else having locked herself in her upstairs apartment until both Barney and I left. I had asked Mouldy to leave us alone and keep the waiter away until Barney and I finished our talk, so he moved off again as soon as the racketeer and I neglected to shake hands with each other.

Seldon waved me to a chair. 'I've heard of you, Mr. Moon,' he said in a tone implying he did not care much for what he had heard. 'Not as a private dick,' he added. 'From Fausta.'

'She tells me about you too,' I said. 'Understand we're rivals.'

He gave me a sharp look. 'What's that supposed to mean?'

'Just an unnecessary crack,' I said. 'What I wanted to talk to you about was Walter Lancaster.'

'Why?' he asked coldly.

'You were here last night, weren't you?'

He shrugged. 'So were a hundred or so other people.'

'But not all of them went out the side door just before Lancaster was shot, and came in again just after.'

His face stiffened and his big brown eyes narrowed. 'Did I do that?'

'A bus boy saw you come in. Fausta doesn't know about it, so don't try to learn from her what bus boy.' I wasn't sure his yen for Fausta would prevent him from taking revenge for squealing, and I didn't want to find out.

'You're a damn liar, Moon,' he said flatly.

'Mr. Moon,' I said.

He shrugged indifferently. 'Mr. Moon, if you prefer. You're still a damn liar. I wasn't away from this table except to get cigarettes.'

'Why'd you have him bumped?' I asked.

For a moment he didn't reply, and when he did his voice could have frozen ice cubes. 'Just from hearing about you, I didn't like you, Mr. Moon. Now that we've met, I realize my first judgment was conservative. Stay away from me and stay away from Fausta, or I'll make you a corpse.'

That was definite enough to be understood. I pushed back my chair, stood up and looked down at him. 'Better bring your gang along to do it, Junior. I was weaned on wilder milk than you.'

He got out of his chair too, and when he started around the table, I thought he was coming after me. But he strode right on past toward the cocktail lounge.

Probably too angry to eat, I thought, and it gave me pleasure to think I might have spoiled his appetite. Then I shrugged, collected my hat from the cloak room, and left.

7

It was six thirty when I left El Patio, and I was beginning to get hungry. But with the time I intended to spend on dinner, it would have been a waste of money to dine at El Patio.

I stopped at a hamburger stand for a sandwich, and was making my next call by seven. It was not a far drive from El Patio, for Willard Knight's home was also on the South Side.

I was rather surprised at the lower-middle-class neighborhood Knight had picked for his home, for while it was not exactly a slum area, it hardly seemed the proper environment for an investment broker. The little frame cottage had no bell, so I pounded on the screen door. The inner door was open because of the heat, and when no one answered my knock, I peered through the screen door just in time to catch a woman peering at me also. She stood in a doorway across the small living room, and the moment my face neared the screen, she faded back out of sight.

Twice more I rapped, and when nothing happened, I tested the screen and found it unlatched. I brought the woman out of her hiding place by slamming it back and forth until it shook the house.

When she suddenly appeared the other side of the screen door, I saw she was squat and middle-aged, in a faded house dress. Her projecting lower lip and flaming eyes may have been generated by my knocking technique, but somehow I catalogued her as the type habitually discourteous to door-to-door salesmen. I could almost read her mind trying to classify me and settling on insurance salesman.

Before she could open her mouth, I said rapidly, 'I'm investigating a murder. If you're Mrs. Knight, I'm looking for your husband.'

Her lower lip remained outthrust, but all expression faded from her eyes and her face paled. After a moment of mental adjustment, she stepped aside and opened the door without saying a word. In her living room I picked a hard sofa as probably the most comfortable of an assortment of cheap furniture and settled myself at one end. Slowly lowering herself to the edge of a straight-backed chair, the woman clasped hands in her lap. Still she did not speak.

'You *are* Mrs. Knight, aren't you?' I asked.

Her head gave a quick, frightened bob. For a woman who spit fire at door-to-door salesmen, she had certainly become a docile lamb.

'Where is your husband, Mrs. Knight?'

Instead of answering, she said in a scared voice, 'What's he done?' Her deep, husky voice surprised me.

I cocked an eyebrow at her. 'Nothing I know of. What do you think he did?'

She said, 'Tell me. You can tell me. I'll have to know anyway. What's he done?' She clasped and unclasped her hands nervously.

'Don't get excited,' I said soothingly. 'A man your husband knew was killed. I'm just making a routine check.'

Her eyes searched mine with suspicion,

then hope. 'You're not after him?'

'I think I've given you the wrong impression. I'm not from the police. I'm a private investigator.' Fishing my license from my wallet, I handed it to her. 'I just want to talk to your husband.'

As she examined the license, some confidence returned to her bearing. 'Moon,' she said, still looking at the license. Then she handed it back to me. 'He's out of town, Mr. Moon. On business.'

'What's his out-of-town address?'

'I don't know.'

I said, 'The information I have which connects your husband with the dead man I got from his secretary. She hasn't told the police. If I can talk to your husband and get a reasonable explanation, maybe the police will never have to know Mr. Knight threatened the murdered man a few hours before the murder. But if I can't, I'll have to give what I know to them and let them pick him up. Do you have a phone?'

Fright showed in her expression again and her hands began to work together. 'I really don't know Willard's address. He said he'd send it.'

'Why'd he leave?'

'I don't know. Something he saw in the papers, I think.'

I didn't say anything, merely continued to look at her. Her lips trembled and she went on. 'He was all right till breakfast. Well, maybe a little grumpy, but not excited like he was after he saw the paper. At first he seemed elated, like the stock market had boomed or something, but when I asked him what the good news was, he looked kind of thoughtful and told me maybe it was a mixed blessing. Then the more he thought about it, the more upset and less glad he seemed. He never did tell me what it was he saw in the paper, just told me to shut up when I asked a second time. Then he packed a suitcase, and told me to phone the office and tell them he had a prospect who would keep him out of town a few days. He phoned a taxi, and when it came he said he'd write me.' Her voice turned faintly bitter. 'I knew he wouldn't tell me any more if I asked, so I never asked.'

'What taxi did he call?'

She shook her head. 'I didn't pay any attention.'

'And you never found out what it was in the paper that upset him?'

'I thought maybe it was something he saw in the financial section, because sometimes he gets upset over stock-market reports. I read over the market list after he left, but I couldn't find anything about any sensational rises or drops in prices.' Her eyes widened at a sudden idea. 'You said a murder. You don't mean the one . . . ' Her voice faded out.

I nodded. 'Yes, I do. Where was your husband last night?'

'At a board meeting.'

'Where?'

'At his company. The Jones and Knight Investment Company.'

My eyes flickered around the room, noting the flimsy wallboard construction and the second-rate furniture. It didn't fit with a man who was one of the two principal stockholders in anything at all. She caught my appraising glance and flushed. 'It's just a small company, and not very old,' she said.

'How long did the meeting last?'

'I don't know. He was gone from six till after one in the morning.'

I rose. 'I guess that covers things. Mind if I use your phone?'

She caught her breath. 'You're not — not going to phone the police?'

'I'm going to phone your husband's partner.' Casually I added, 'Jones flew to Kansas City last night. Seems funny he'd do that on the night of a board meeting, doesn't it?'

Her face went pale. Without a word, she rose and led me through a narrow dining room into a back hall where a phone sat on a table. In the telephone book I found a residence listing for Harlan Jones and dialed the number. A female with an intriguingly throaty voice answered. When I asked for Jones, she said, 'Just a moment, please.' There was a suggestive croon to the voice which built interesting pictures in my mind.

I stared at the hall's dim wallpaper design until a pompous voice said in my ear, 'Jones speaking.'

'Manville Moon,' I said. 'I'm trying to locate your partner.'

'Sorry, Mr. Moon. Knight is out of town. May I help you?'

'Out of town?' I repeated. 'Did he present my proposition at your board meeting last night?'

'Board meeting?' He sounded puzzled.

'Didn't you have a board meeting last night?'

'No . . . ' he said slowly. 'I wasn't even in town last night, Mr. Moon. But I don't quite understand what you mean anyway. We have no board of directors. We're not incorporated. Knight and I are sole owners. What was your proposition?'

I hung up quietly.

Mrs. Knight's squat figure was centered in the dining-room door. Her hands rigidly clasped each other and fright peered from the back of her eyes. All I did was look at her without any expression on my face, but she backed into the dining room as though terrified.

I followed her without hurry. 'Where is he?' I asked in an easy voice.

'I don't know! Honest I don't!' Then

words tumbled from her in a deep-toned stream. 'I don't know where he goes. He says board meetings and comes in at all hours, and I know it's not board meetings because his company has no board. But it isn't drinking either. I've smelled his breath after he's asleep. I don't know where he goes or what he does.' She stopped with fat shoulders pressed against a wall. Her frightened face tilted upward, and she licked trembling lips.

I said, 'Don't you ask where he goes?'

'I couldn't. If you knew his temper, you'd see I couldn't. All I know is he makes good money, but we never have anything. If I said right out I didn't believe his board meetings, he'd — he'd kill me, like as not.' Then her eyes grew even wider and the back of one hand pressed against her mouth. 'He wouldn't really,' she whispered. 'He wouldn't kill anybody.'

I looked down at her thoughtfully until two tears seeped from the corners of her eyes and dribbled across her cheeks. Then suddenly I felt infinitely sorry for her and a little ashamed of myself. I said, 'Take it easy, Mrs. Knight. Your husband may be able to explain the whole thing.'

She shook her head. 'You'll tell the police. I know you will. And they'll arrest him for something he didn't do.'

Her shoulders hunched and she bowed her head into upturned palms as sobs began to shake her body. As quietly as I could, I got my hat from the front room and left, feeling somewhat like a heel.

From a drugstore booth I phoned Warren Day at his home. 'How does this sound?' I asked. 'Three hours before Lancaster got it, a guy threatened to fix him. The guy's wife says he has a temper, and he wasn't where he told his wife he was at the time of the murder. Also, he's taken a powder.'

Day said, 'Who's the guy?'

'Willard Knight. Jones and Knight Investments.' I told him the same story the secretary-bookkeeper had told me. 'He's the kind of guy who invests all his money in stock and lives in a five-thousand-dollar shack.'

'Where's the shack?'

I told him the address.

'I'll have Hannegan get a picture from his wife and we'll send out the word. That all?'

'All for now.'

'Okay. Goodbye.'

'You're welcome,' I said.

'Huh? Oh, you mean you want thanks. Listen, Moon, I been off duty for hours and I was watching a television show. I should thank you for pulling me away from Hopalong Cassidy?'

His receiver slammed in my ear.

8

Harlan Jones's house was on Park Lane over on the West Side. It was a modest but substantial place, alone in the fifteen-thousand-dollar class. I contrasted the broad, well-kept lawn and solidly built brick bungalow with Willard Knight's strip of unkempt yard and his flimsy frame house. Before ever seeing him I bet that Mr. Jones never took fliers on the market.

It was just eight p.m. when I pushed the button next to the front door. The woman who answered my ring was as much a contrast to Mrs. Knight as her home was to the Knight home. Sleek and serene, she escaped thinness by that slight margin stylists call willowy, which is between slender and skinny. Golden hair pushed back from a broad unlined brow in careful waves. Her eyes were wide-spaced and green, and her nose arched slightly but delicately over a soft, humorous mouth. She looked thirty, but by the barely discernible crow's-feet at her eye corners, I judged her a well-preserved thirty-five.

I said, 'Mrs. Jones?'

'Yes.' It was the same throaty voice I had heard over the phone.

'Mr. Jones in?'

'Not at the moment. He just stepped down to the drugstore, but he'll be right back. Will you come in?'

I said, 'Thanks,' and let her lead me into a tastefully furnished living room equipped with modern furniture which was neither new nor worn, but had an air of much comfortable use.

'I'm Manville Moon,' I explained when we were settled in easy chairs with a knee-high glass-topped table between us. 'I phoned earlier.'

'Oh, yes,' she said. 'I answered the phone.' She laughed lightly. 'Harlan will be glad to see you. He was upset when you hung up on him.' Her tone grew an edge of tolerant cynicism. 'Harlan is always upset when he thinks he's lost a chance to make a nickel.' Then, apparently realizing her flippancy was not exactly diplomatic with one of her husband's prospects, she looked contrite. 'I shouldn't say that. I'm always saying things I shouldn't.'

'It won't hurt your husband's business,' I said dryly. 'I'm afraid I left a wrong impression with Mr. Jones. I'm not in the market for stocks and bonds.' Fishing out my wallet, I handed my license over for examination for the third time that day. She read it carefully, then looked at me with an amused quirk lifting the corners of her mouth.

'A detective! How dramatic! Don't tell me Harlan is secretly a criminal.'

I shook my head. 'My interest isn't in your husband.'

'Neither is mine,' she said frankly, then colored to the roots of her hair and emitted a throaty little laugh. 'Don't I say the damnedest things?'

I smiled.

'You're nice when you grin,' she said. 'Sort of like a friendly Saint Bernard whose face has been chewed by a bulldog. Do you mind my saying that? You must know you're not exactly handsome. But of course with those shoulders, you don't have to be.'

As she seemed to require only occasional answers when carrying on a conversation, I contented myself with merely continuing to grin.

'Are you interested in *me?*' she asked suddenly.

'How do you mean? As a detective?'

'How else?' Then her eyes widened and she let out a healthy, spontaneous laugh. 'Are you interested some other way? That might be fun.'

'I came to see your husband about his partner,' I explained.

All laughter faded from her eyes. 'Willard?'

I nodded, mildly intrigued by her use of Knight's first name.

'What's he done?' Her tone was intently serious.

I shrugged. 'Nothing I know of. Except disappear.'

She studied me carefully and a faint trace of amusement reappeared in her eyes. 'Going out of town on business is hardly disappearing.' Then she frowned. 'At least, Harlan *said* he was away on business.'

I remained silent.

'Harlan never lies. To me, anyway. I'd catch him in a minute.' Continuing to eye me, her tone gathered impatience. 'What do you want to know about Willard?'

'Where he is. I want to talk to him.'

She tightened her lips. 'Is it a secret?' she asked finally.

'No, but I'd just as soon hold it till your husband comes home and not have to repeat myself.'

She fell silent and thought wrinkles momentarily marred the smoothness of her brow. Then, lifting her shoulders deprecatingly, she said, 'Will you have a drink?'

I nodded assent. 'Been waiting for an offer.'

Her good humor returned at once. 'You should have asked.' She rose and moved toward the hall, stopping in the doorway long enough to remark, 'I forget everything else when I'm talking. I talk too much, don't I?'

'Probably,' I said. 'But it's fun listening.'

She laughed and continued toward the back of the house. Immediately she returned. 'What do you drink?' she asked.

'What do you have?'

'Beer. Bourbon. Scotch.'

Without rye as a choice, I have no preference. But for some reason, possibly because the whole atmosphere surrounding Mrs. Jones was slightly mad, a slightly mad mixture I had not tasted for years popped into my mind. 'Half a shot of bourbon, half a shot of Scotch, and plain water,' I said.

Her eyes widened. Then she laughed delightedly like a child with a new toy and returned to the kitchen. She had been gone about two minutes when I heard the front door open and close again. A round little fat man carrying a carton of cigarettes came in from the hall. He stopped short when he saw me, then advanced diffidently.

I got out of my chair. 'You Mr. Jones?'

'Yes.'

'Manville Moon,' I said, sticking out my hand. 'I phoned earlier.'

'Oh, yes, Mr. Moon.' He pumped my hand delightedly, and I got the impression he was quickly appraising the cut of my clothes in an attempt to size up my bankroll.

'I took advantage of you over the phone,' I said. 'I'm not in the market for stocks. I just wanted some fast information about Willard Knight.' For the fourth time I passed over my license.

His eyes grew round. 'Private investigator,' he said uncomprehendingly. 'I don't understand.'

Mrs. Knight came back into the room, bearing a tray with two glasses. 'Are you back, Harlan? This is Mr. Moon. He's a private eye. Isn't that exciting?'

I winced, as I always do when anyone calls me a private eye.

'Yes,' Jones started to say. 'We've — '

'We're having a new drink,' she interrupted. 'Scotch and bourbon mixed. Go make yourself one.'

'I don't want a drink,' Jones said petulantly.

'Suit yourself.' She handed me one of the glasses, took the other herself, and curled up in a chair with her legs under her.

Easing myself back into my own chair, I said, 'Luck,' and tried a sip of the drink. It did not taste like it had before. In fact it tasted lousy.

'That's wonderful!' Mrs. Jones thrilled after her first sip. 'Wherever did you discover it?'

'It was invented on the Continent,' I said with a straight face.

'See here,' Jones put in suddenly. 'What's all this private investigator business about?' He laid down his carton of cigarettes and seated himself on the couch. Immediately he picked up the carton again, broke it open and stripped the cellophane from a pack. 'Cigarette?' he asked.

'No, thanks,' I said; then to Mrs. Jones, 'Mind cigar smoke?'

'Love it. I like to see a man smoke a cigar.'

After politely holding a match for Jones and lighting up myself, I abruptly got to the point of my visit. I said, 'I'm here about the murder that took place last night, Mr. Jones.'

'Isn't he dramatic?' his wife asked. Then her face stiffened and she said in a strangely hushed voice, 'Not Willard?'

'He means Walter Lancaster, I presume,' Jones told her with mild impatience. To me he said, 'I've already told the police everything I know about the man. What is it you want with me?'

'I want you to tell me where Knight is.'

He looked surprised and a little relieved. 'I don't know. Our secretary phoned his wife this morning when he didn't come in, and Mrs. Knight said he left town to see a prospect. She didn't seem to know where he went. Why don't you ask her?'

'I did. She doesn't know either.'

Mrs. Jones said, 'No doubt he'll wire in tomorrow. Can't you wait?'

'No, he won't wire,' I said. 'He's run.'

Nervously, Jones punched out his cigarette. 'I don't understand this, Mr. Moon. Is Knight suspected of the crime?'

I shrugged. 'Not exactly. But a few hours before the murder he threatened Lancaster, and now he's dropped out of sight. When his wife last saw him, he was in a peculiar hurry. And he definitely was not where he told his wife he was last night. You established that on the phone.'

Mrs. Jones said, 'Willard couldn't have. Why he was . . . ' Her voice trailed off and she finished lamely, 'You have mentioned he has a temper though, haven't you, Harlan?' Abruptly she rose, excused herself and left the room.

Jones said, 'This is all a great shock to me, Mr. Moon. But I'm sure my partner wouldn't kill anyone. There must be some other explanation for his absence.'

'I haven't accused him of murder,' I said. 'I merely want to find him. And since you know his habits, maybe you can give me a lead. Where would he go to hide out?'

'Hide out? I haven't the faintest idea.'

'He have a summer camp or a cottage anywhere?'

'No. I'm sure he hasn't.'

'Have friends in other cities?'

He thought for a while. 'No one special I can think of,' he said finally. 'But I suppose he has some out-of-town friends.'

Mrs. Jones came back into the room carrying a single drink. 'I fixed you one of the new drinks,' she told her husband, handing him the glass.

He accepted it as though he didn't want it, but didn't know how to refuse before company. As Mrs. Jones passed between us on the way back to her chair, she casually dropped a note in my lap, her body hiding the movement from her husband. Without looking down, I let one palm fall across it.

'You seem to know Knight as well as your husband does,' I said to Mrs. Jones. 'Any idea where he'd hole up if he didn't want to be found?'

'I'm sure Harlan knows him much better than I,' she said in a suddenly prim tone. 'I know him only as my husband's partner.'

'All right. As your husband's partner, where would he go to hide?'

'I'm sure I have no idea.'

I got out of my chair, slipping the note in my pocket as I rose. 'I won't keep you any longer. Thanks for the drink.' The drink stood, practically untouched, on the little cocktail table.

Jones said, 'I'm afraid we haven't helped much.'

'You've been fine,' I said politely, and bowed my way out.

9

A block from the house I pulled my car over to the curb, switched on the dome light, and read the note Mrs. Jones had dropped in my lap. It said: 'Meet me at the Sheridan Lounge at eleven p.m.' Nothing more, not even a signature. My wristwatch said a quarter of nine, and the Sheridan Lounge is in the basement of the Sheridan Hotel, just two blocks from where I was parked.

I frowned down at the note, mildly irritated by its terseness. I was in no mood for clandestine romance, if that was what the woman had in mind. But if she had some information about Knight, I could hardly afford to stand her up. Her tone had seemed over-insistent when she said, 'I know him only as my husband's partner,' which might indicate she knew something she was unwilling to disclose in front of Mr. Jones, or might merely be one of the oddly vapid utterances she routinely made without apparent thought.

Resignedly, I decided the only way to find out was to be at the Sheridan Lounge at eleven. And since I had not taken time to so much as wash my hands and face since I left my flat at one, I decided to employ the two and a quarter hours before my date to wash and change my shirt.

As no garage comes with my flat, I keep my Plymouth at a public garage up the street. At nine I put my car away for the night and started to walk to my apartment, deciding to take a taxi for my date. I can only drive a car so long before the strain on my thigh muscles caused by operating the accelerator with my false foot begins to cause my thigh to ache.

As I passed the areaway between my place and the building next door, a dim figure stepped from between the buildings and a hand flash shone in my face. Immediately it flicked out again. 'Night watchman,' explained a cheery voice.

Peering through the gloom, I made out a big, chunkily built man with a battered but good-natured face. 'You must be new,' I said. 'What's the matter with Jim?'

'Sick. You're Mr. Moon, aren't you?'

'Yes.'

Idly I wondered why he wasn't in uniform, since the block's regular night watchman was a deputized member of the force. I should also have wondered how he knew my name, but his cheery manner threw me off guard.

The man touched his cloth cap. 'Bit dark tonight. Evening, sir.'

'Night,' I said, and walked on two steps.

What felt like a baseball bat, but was probably the flashlight, caught me behind the ear. I didn't black out; I only lost the ability to control my arms and legs. Falling forward, I landed on hands and knees, and when a big hand grasped my collar and dragged me into the areaway, I was powerless to do anything about it.

Leaning me against the side of the building in a sitting position, the big man peered down at me with a grin. I gazed up at him, stunned, and unable to move either arm.

'I ain't gonna kill you,' the man said.

'Just make you even uglier than you are. And when you wake up, remember to stay out of Barney Seldon's hair. Got that?'

My head lolled forward.

'I guess you got it,' he decided. 'Now I'll learn you how to kick a field goal.' Tentatively he swung his right foot to limber it up, and added, 'Your head is the ball.'

Apparently he was satisfied that he was in kicking shape. With a kind of morbid fascination I watched his foot swing back and his body lean forward to balance it.

My eyes were fixed on the foot, and as it reached the peak of its backswing, a hand snaked from the darkness and clamped about the ankle. The foot went even higher than it intended, the fake watchman's mouth popped open in surprise, and he fell flat on his face. Before he could scramble as far as his hands and knees, a long lanky form settled in the middle of his back and the new arrival slashed downward with the edge of one palm.

Farmer Cole arose, ran his tongue along the edge of his buckteeth, and regarded me without expression. 'He got you with a rabbit punch,' he said. 'Paralyzed, aren't you?'

I managed a thick, 'Yes.'

'It'll pass in a minute.'

He stood watching both of us without any particular interest, until feeling began to return to my limbs. When my arms and legs would again work, I felt the lump behind my ear and shakily climbed to my feet. Unreasonably, I felt irritation rather than gratitude at the Farmer's sudden appearance. 'You been tailing me?' I asked.

'How do you think I got here?' he said in a bored voice.

This only increased my unreasonable anger. I had always been proud of possessing almost a sixth sense about being tailed, but I had not had an inkling of a suspicion that the Farmer was within miles. Suddenly remembering the equally timely appearance he had made in Carson City, I realized he had been right behind me all day.

'When I need a nursemaid, I'll let you know,' I said between clenched teeth.

He glanced down at the still-unconscious strong-arm man, raised one eyebrow, and shrugged. 'Boss's orders, bud. Personally I don't care who busts you up. Wouldn't mind doing it myself.'

'That I'd like to see,' I said, staggering forward and thrusting out my jaw.

'Okay,' he obliged, planting either a right or a left hook on it. I am not sure which because I didn't see it.

When I was able to get to my feet the second time, Farmer Cole was nowhere in sight. Shaking the cobwebs out of my brain, I frisked my first assailant, who had progressed to the point of groaning and rolling over on his back.

The guy had come prepared for any contingency. Removing from his pockets a gun, a clasp knife, a set of brass knuckles and a sap, I stacked them in a neat pile a dozen feet away. When I returned, he was sitting up and rubbing the back of his neck.

I waited until he had fully recovered his faculties and was on his feet. I figured the blow from Farmer Cole's edged palm had about the same effect on him the flashlight had had on me, and his head must be throbbing with about the same intensity as mine. The right (or left) hook I had taken from the Farmer made the punishment I had absorbed more than the fake watchman's, however, a matter I felt it necessary to rectify.

He glanced around carefully and asked, 'Where's the other guy?'

'Gone,' I said. 'There's just you and me.'

He allowed a delighted smile to form on his battered lips. 'How come you didn't take off too?'

'Curiosity,' I told him. 'I want to see if you can do it when my back isn't turned.'

He shook his head wonderingly. 'I'm almost ashamed to do it, bud. I got thirty pounds on you, and I used to be a professional.'

'So was I,' I admitted modestly.

'Aw, let's call it off,' he said. 'Shake on it.'

He stuck out a huge right, I grinned and pretended to reach for it. Instantly his left whistled toward my head; I stepped inside, pushed a right jab into his belly, and followed with a left uppercut and right and left hooks to the jaw in rapid succession.

In his prime he couldn't have been more than a tanker, and now he was getting soft. On the other hand, I had once been fairly hot in the ring. Not nearly as hot as I thought at the time, now that I look back on it, but nevertheless better than the average club fighter. In spite of a false leg I still have most of my coordination, and it was no match. He was staggering like a drunk after the first flurry.

Ordinarily I am not sadistic, but Barney Seldon had ordered his goon to leave permanent marks, and I felt the least I could do in return was leave temporary ones. I could have put him away with the second hook, but I kept him awake and deliberately cut him to ribbons.

When he was ready for the hospital, I went up to my apartment and called a police ambulance. Then, while waiting for the ambulance to arrive, I phoned Warren Day again.

'Are you going to keep this up all night?' he demanded. 'I don't work on the night shift.'

'How does this strike you?' I asked, ignoring his complaint. 'This evening before I called you the first time, I questioned Barney Seldon about the Lancaster killing. A little while ago one of his goons tried to beat me up.'

'How do you know it was his goon?'

'He took pains to inform me before he went to work. It was supposed to scare me out of Barney's hair.'

'Hmm,' the inspector said. 'Think I'll talk to Barney again. Where's the goon?'

'Outside waiting for an ambulance.'

'You preferring charges?'

'You're damn right,' I said. 'Against both the goon and Barney. We have enough local hoods to worry about without letting a couple of out-of-town punks get away with anything.'

'Fine,' he said, pleased with me for a change. 'I'll have Barney picked up if he's still in town, and you can swear out a complaint in the morning.'

I knew what pleased him, and it wasn't

my sentiments about out-of-towners. He was simply glad of an excuse to hold the mobster while he worked him over about the Lancaster killing.

I said, 'You haven't inquired about my damages. If I didn't know you regarded me practically as a foster son, I'd suspect you weren't worried.'

Day grunted. 'Where'd you get hit?'

'In the head. Twice.'

'Then there's nothing to worry about,' he growled, and hung up.

10

I stood at the bar in the Sheridan from ten of eleven until a quarter after, and was about to forget the whole thing and leave when Mrs. Jones came in from the street door. Smiling in my direction, she made straight for a corner table. I moved over from the bar and joined her.

'I'm late,' she said brightly.

'Yes. I noticed.'

Curiously, she eyed the black and blue mark which had formed on my chin. 'What happened to your face?'

'I had to break another date to get here. The woman was angry.'

She grinned at me. 'You got off easy. Break a date with me sometime and see what happens to you.'

A white-coated waiter glided over to our table and bent from the waist, then waited soundlessly. Mrs. Jones said, 'Half a shot of Scotch, half a shot of bourbon, and water. Two of them.'

'One of them,' I corrected. 'And a rye and water.'

When the waiter moved off, I said, 'Well, Mrs. Jones?'

'Don't be so formal. My name's Isobel.'

'All right. Isobel. How'd you get out of the house?'

'Walked out. Harlan goes to bed on the stroke of ten, and an earthquake couldn't wake him. We have separate rooms, so if I leave the house after ten thirty, he never knows it.' She laughed aloud, enjoying her cleverness. 'What he doesn't know won't hurt him.'

The waiter brought our drinks and neither of us spoke until he departed again. Then I asked, 'What's on your mind, Isobel?'

She looked at me archly. 'What's on *your* mind?'

'Sleep, mainly,' I said dryly. 'But I can spare a few minutes.'

She pouted. 'If you're going to be mean, I wish I hadn't come.'

'I'm not being mean. But I assume you have something to tell me, or you wouldn't be here. Spill it and I'll be playful with you afterward.'

'How playful?'

I said cautiously, 'As much as you can be in a place as public as the Sheridan Lounge.'

'Don't you have an apartment?'

'Yes,' I admitted. 'But it's only one room and my poor old mother is a light sleeper.'

'Oh.' She sounded disappointed.

'So what's on your mind?' I asked again.

Reluctantly she brought her thoughts around to business. 'It's about Willard Knight.'

I waited.

'You're wasting your time looking for him. He couldn't possibly have killed that man last night.'

I waited for more, but apparently no more was forthcoming.

'Look, Isobel,' I said finally. 'You're a nice gal in an unbalanced sort of way, and I'd enjoy wasting time with you if I wasn't busy looking for a killer. What do you expect me to do now? Say thanks very much and forget Knight?'

She nodded vigorously. 'I'm sure he's innocent.'

'Why? Do you know where he was last night?'

'I know he wasn't near that night club.'

'How do you know? Were you with him?'

She looked offended. 'If you're intimating I'd have an affair with anyone,' she said with illogical virtue, 'I'll have you know I'm a respectable married woman. I just *know* Willard Knight wouldn't commit murder.'

At that moment a tall, shaggy-haired man with a gaunt Lincoln-esque face entered the bar from the hotel's downstairs hall. Isobel emitted a small shriek when she saw him. I looked at her inquiringly, noticing her face lose color.

'What's the matter?'

'That man!' She faltered, then went on. 'I know him. I mean, he knows me. He'll see us together.'

I glanced over at the man, who was approaching the bar. 'And tell your husband?'

'No, not that. I mean yes, he'll tell my husband.' She was so agitated, she didn't know what she meant.

When the man reached the bar, he turned and glanced casually around the room. His eyes stopped at our table, blazed with amazement, and at once he moved directly toward us. He kept his gaze unwaveringly on Isobel's face until the edge of our table prevented him from getting any closer to her.

'What are you doing here?' he asked harshly.

Isobel's face had turned dead white. 'This — this is Mr. Moon. George Smith, Mr. Moon.'

I looked him over. 'Sit down and have a drink, George.'

Paying no attention to me, he repeated, 'What are you doing here?'

Isobel said desperately, 'Mr. Moon and I are having a business meeting. It's — well, he's a private detective.'

Smith's eyes swung sharply down at me. He gave me a thorough examination, shifted his glance back at Isobel, and comprehension broke over his face.

'Hired by your husband, was he?' he asked, and when she simply looked at him blankly, added, 'And now he's offering to sell you the data he's collected instead of turning it over to your husband.'

I said in a bored tone, 'Back off of that one fast, buster, or you'll find your teeth all over the floor.'

Isobel didn't even know what we were talking about. In a bewildered voice she said, 'Mr. Moon is hunting a murderer. That Lancaster affair that was in all the papers. I'm just one of hundreds of witnesses he's questioning.'

Again Smith looked down at me. 'Hundreds, eh? You question them all in night clubs?'

'About the blackmail crack,' I reminded him. 'Take all the time you want to apologize. Anything up to three seconds.'

He started to form a sneer on his face, then changed his mind and said indifferently, 'I withdraw the remark. Nice seeing you again, Isobel. Give my regards to what's-his-name, your husband.' Without another word he turned and left the room by the same way he had entered.

'Queer friends you have,' I remarked.

Isobel was sliding from her chair, collecting her bag and gloves as she moved. 'Let's get out of here,' she said.

Dropping two dollar bills on the table, I followed her through the street exit. She made straight for a cab standing at the curb, glancing nervously over her shoulder once before climbing through the door I held open.

'Where to?' I asked when I had joined her.

'Anywhere. Just so it's far.'

To the cabdriver I said, 'Straight ahead three blocks.'

'You sending me home?' she asked as we pulled away.

'Yeah.'

She looked once through the taxi's rear window; then, seeming to regain composure, leaned her head against my shoulder. 'Don't send me home,' she said.

'It's nearly midnight.'

'Let's at least ride for a while.'

I shrugged, then said to the driver, 'Keep going and swing through Midland Park. And don't rush.'

We both remained silent as the cab rolled along Park Lane. What she was thinking about, I don't know, but I was thinking I had wasted an evening. Isobel Jones gradually was taking form in my mind as a woman who grabbed at every passing man she saw. I was relatively certain she had been having some kind of an affair with Willard Knight, for she did not impress me as the type of woman who would go to the defense of a man merely because he was her husband's partner. And it also seemed certain the character we had just left at the Sheridan was, or had been, a man in her life. Possibly, judging from her agitation at seeing him, one she was trying to ditch.

To clinch it, she was making a mild pass at me. Women don't pass at men with faces like mine unless they are in the habit of instinctively making passes at every man.

We crossed Mason Avenue and moved slowly along the sweepingly curved drives of the park. It was a moonless night, but brilliant starlight barely prevented it from being pitch-black.

'Put your arm around me,' she demanded.

I put my arm around her.

She turned up her face and closed her eyes. Her lips pursed expectantly, and I grinned down at her until she finally popped her eyes open. She looked cross when she saw my grin. 'Kiss me,' she said sharply.

I gave her a short, careless kiss, then pushed her erect and removed my arm. 'Look me up between murders.'

She watched me uncertainly, chewing her lower lip. 'Take me home,' she decided suddenly.

The cabdriver half-turned in his seat. 'Car without lights following.'

Craning to peer through the rear window, I saw it about a half block back. It kept the same distance while I watched it for two more blocks.

'Want me to lose him?' our driver asked.

'No. Take the lady home.'

The rest of the trip we made in silence. Isobel periodically glanced through the rear window at our shadow, her face nervous and her brow puckered thought-fully.

As we neared her home, she asked the driver to let her out at the corner. Getting out first, I held the door for her. Our tail, suddenly switching on his lights, rolled past as though he had no interest in our doings. It was a taxicab.

'That must be your friend, George,' I said to Isobel. 'What's on his mind?'

She shook her head. 'I've no idea.'

She watched the taxi's taillight until it disappeared around the next corner, then abruptly said goodbye and nearly ran toward her house. I got in the front seat with the driver and told him the address of my flat.

As we turned into Grand Avenue, the cabdriver said, 'Our friend's with us again.'

'Let him enjoy himself.'

I didn't even bother to look around. When we reached my flat, the trailing taxi pulled in right behind us, his bumper nearly against ours. As I paid off my driver, I watched from the side of my eyes and saw George Smith step from the other cab. My driver pulled away and I waited for George to make a move. But when he merely glowered from under shaggy brows, I grinned at him and started up the walk toward the apartment-house door.

George caught up just as I reached it. I held the door for him to follow me into the lobby, then faced him, waiting. His angry eyes burned up and down my frame as though he were calculating his chances. They halted at my jawline, and suddenly he swung.

My knees bent just enough so that his fist skimmed off my hat. A short left jab into his exposed ribs swooshed the air out of him. Then I snapped erect, crashed a right hook to his jaw, and he spun like a top. The second time around he pitched forward and I caught him in my arms. I lowered him gently to a seated position with his back against the wall.

When he returned to this world, I was seated on the lowest steps puffing a cigar. He wagged his head a few times, felt his jaw and focused his eyes at me with difficulty.

'Sleep well?' I asked.

He eyed me with distaste. 'I ought to

knock your block off.'

I blew smoke at him. 'You can keep trying. But you'll only end up punchy. What's your grudge?'

Struggling to his feet, he groped for the outer door handle to hold himself up. 'Stay away from Isobel,' he said.

'Why?'

He leaned toward me, nearly lost his balance, and recovered. 'Because I'll beat your brains out if you go near her again.' His eyes burned with an emotion I suddenly realized was jealousy.

'Why, you're in love with her, aren't you?' I asked softly.

'That's none of your business,' he snarled, and pushing through the door, was gone.

11

I stayed in bed until almost noon.

I always find myself doing leg work at midnight when I get on a case. Any cops working on the same case knock off at five, go home and forget about it until the next morning, when they start off bright and early again. But not night-owl Moon. I have to stay up half the night, with the result that it is noon before I can get started again.

When I had showered, shaved and put away some eggs and coffee, I phoned Warren Day at Headquarters. 'I assume you haven't caught up with Barney Seldon,' I said, 'or you'd have been after me to come down and swear out a complaint.'

'Apparently he scooted back across the river before his goon jumped you,' he growled. 'I doubt that he'll come back as long as we hold the goon, but you'd better come down and sign the complaint anyway.'

'How about extradition?'

The inspector snorted. 'On an assault charge? With the lawyers he's got? We'd get hold of him about Christmas.'

'Where's the goon?' I asked.

'City Hospital. His name's Percival Sweet, incidentally.'

'It's what?' I asked incredulously.

'Percival Sweet. And it's no phony. He had an Illinois permit to carry a gun on him.'

I told him I would be down later to swear out complaints against Barney Seldon and Percival Sweet, and hung up.

The day started to become inauspicious when I arrived at City Hospital. Immediately I got myself wound up to the neck in red tape.

It started when the middle-aged woman in the registrar's office told me Percival Sweet was in ward sixteen. Then, as I started to walk away, she called after me, 'But I don't think you can see him.'

Coming back, I looked at the sign on the wall over her head, which stated visiting hours were one to two and seven to eight, checked my watch against the wall clock, noting both read two minutes after one, and asked, 'Why?'

'Ward sixteen is the prison ward. You have to have permission.'

'From whom?'

She looked uncertain. 'Maybe you better see the chief nurse,' she suggested. 'Unless you've got some kind of legal paper.'

I admitted that I didn't have some kind of legal paper.

'Usually visitors up there do,' she confided. 'Things like habeas corpus and so on. Mostly the visitors are lawyers.'

The chief nurse, similarly stumped by my lack of a legal paper, shunted me off to the chief of staff, who passed me on to the hospital superintendent. By the time I reached the latter's office, I was getting mad.

'Look, Doctor,' I started to say.

'Not doctor,' he corrected. 'I'm not a physician.'

He was a thin, precise man with gold-rimmed glasses and an air of waiting for someone to hand him papers to sign. A discreet desk marker announced his name as M. M. Witherspoon.

'All right,' I said. 'Mister, then. I'm trying to see a patient, but all I get is the run-around.'

He glanced at his watch. 'Visiting hours are on now. See the registrar. Room one hundred.'

I said, 'I've seen the registrar. I've seen the chief nurse. I've seen the chief of staff.' I drew a chair from next to his desk, sat in it and stretched out my legs. 'You have any influence around here, Mr. Witherspoon?'

'I beg your pardon?'

Sliding my license across his desk, I said, 'I want to talk to a patient named Percival Sweet. He was brought in with multiple contusions last night. He's under arrest in ward sixteen.'

His eyes raised from the license to my face. 'I know the case.' He glanced back at the license, said, 'Private detective,' and looked up again. 'Sorry, Mr. Moon. You'll have to have police permission.'

Retrieving my license, I politely asked to use his desk phone, and when he granted permission with equal politeness,

I told the switchboard operator to get me Homicide. 'Get me either Inspector Day or Lieutenant Hannegan,' I said.

Warren Day came to the phone. 'Yeah?' he growled.

'Moon,' I said. 'I'm in the superintendent's office at City Hospital. Will you tell him it's all right for me to see Percy?'

'Can't get in, eh?'

'Oh, sure, I can get in. I phoned to tell you I can get in.'

He laughed, apparently in one of his pixie moods. 'Let me talk to the superintendent.'

I passed the phone over to M. M. Witherspoon, who listened for a minute, said, 'All right, Inspector,' and dropped the instrument back on its cradle.

Ripping a sheet from a three-by-five pad on his desk, the superintendent scribbled a few words on it and pushed it toward me. The note authorized me to visit Percival Sweet in ward sixteen.

An overage cop named Mike Sullivan was on sentry duty in front of the barred entrance to ward sixteen. He sat tilted against the wall in a straight-backed chair reading a detective magazine. I thought Mike had long ago retired, since he had walked a beat in my neighborhood when I was in grammar school, and on more than one occasion I had felt his night stick across the seat of my pants for stealing apples.

As I approached, he looked up from his magazine and said in a pleased tone, 'Hello, Manny.'

'How are you, Mike? Thought you'd retired.'

'Next month,' he said. 'Ain't this a fine detail to end with after thirty years?'

'Somebody's got to do it.' I handed him my pass. 'If I'd known you were back here, I wouldn't have gone through all the rigmarole of getting this.'

He raised his eyes from the scribbled note. 'You wouldn't have got in without it. With only twenty-three days to go, I ain't breaking any regulations.'

Drawing a key from his pocket, he unlocked the door and followed me through it, carefully relocking it from the inside.

The room was clean and airy, and except for the barred windows and door, looked like any other sick ward. Of the dozen beds arranged foot to head alongside the inside wall, only two were occupied. One contained an old man with red-flecked eyes and the rasping cough of a chronic alcoholic. Percival Sweet occupied the second bunk beyond his.

With the head of his hospital bed cranked up to form a back rest, the ex-pugilist sat half-erect, his spine cushioned against a pillow. One eye was swollen shut, a piece of sticking plaster bridged his nose, and the rest of his face was a mottled purple and yellow. As we neared the bed, he drew thick lips back over large yellow teeth in a snarl.

'How you feeling, Percy?' I asked.

'None of your damned business!'

I clucked my tongue. 'It's not my fault you're a washout as a hood. Why don't you try another profession?'

He glowered at me without making any reply. I sat on the vacant bed next to his and let my feet dangle. 'Don't they have nurses in this ward?' I asked Mike.

'When they want a nurse, I have to get one. I got them trained not to ask between regular rounds.'

Feeling in my breast pocket, I found I had just four cigars. 'All right to smoke in here?' I asked Mike.

He shrugged. 'The patients do, when they got tobacco.'

I handed one of the cigars to Mike, tossed another over Percy to the old man, who caught it with the skill of an inveterate butt sniper, and offered a third to Percy. In the back of his eyes disdain fought a heroic battle with tobacco hunger, but lost. He accepted as though doing me a favor.

After setting fire to my own cigar and Percy's, I tossed the match folder onto the old man's bed. Mike used one of his own matches. Percy leaned back and greedily drew his lungs full of smoke, then let it roll slowly through his nostrils.

I said, 'You're out of smokes, eh?'

He drew again on the cigar without answering.

I said, 'Of course, you won't need smokes where you're going.'

A deepening of creases between his eyes was the only evidence of attention to my last remark. I pretended absorbed interest in my cigar ash while I let him think it over. For a full minute the room was silent as Percy turned my remark over in his mind, Mike and the old vagrant concentrating on nothing but their cigars, and I amusing myself by swinging my feet.

Finally Percy rose to the bait. 'Okay, shamus. Where am I going?'

'The name is Mister Moon,' I said.

'I've heard that gag about you. You like to work guys over who don't call you Mister.'

'Not guys,' I said. 'Just hoods. Guys can call me anything they want.'

'So suppose I tell you to go to hell? You gonna work over a hospital patient in front of a cop?'

'There's always the chance you'll beat this rap,' I said. 'Then I'd look you up. Of course, your chance of beating it is pretty slim, so you wouldn't be risking much.'

He studied a smoke ring he had blown until it disintegrated, then asked, 'Where am I going, Mr. Moon?'

'To the gas chamber, of course.'

'For assault and battery?' He let out a

laugh intended to be derisive, but it wavered slightly at the end.

Sliding off the bed, I picked up my hat. 'Well,' I said briskly, 'I just dropped in to see how you were taking it. I have to hand it to you. You're certainly a cool guy.' I started to move toward the door.

'Just a minute!' Percy called.

I stopped and half-turned toward him. He watched me uneasily, half-suspicious that I was merely throwing out bait. 'Just what in hell are you talking about?'

'The Lancaster killing, of course. Have you bumped so many guys, you don't know which one you're taking the count for?'

From his expression it was hard to determine whether he was disturbed or not. His mouth tightened and his visible eye became more wary, but that was all. 'What's your rush?' he asked. 'Sit down for a minute.'

After frowning at my watch, I shrugged, returned to my former seat, and waited for him to resume conversation. Eventually he asked, 'What about the Lancaster killing?'

'Hasn't anyone from Homicide been here yet?'

149

He shook his head. 'Just one regular cop this morning.'

'I thought they'd have been here long ago.' Checking my watch again, I turned on an astonished expression. 'It's two hours since Barney Seldon broke. I wouldn't have come over, but I thought you'd surely know about it by now.' Suddenly I looked concerned. 'Maybe I better shut up before I tell something Inspector Day doesn't want let out.'

At mention of Barney Seldon, Percy's face had become expressionless. 'The boss broke, huh?'

I nodded. 'If I were you, I'd get a smart lawyer and shift the blame right back on him. If you establish that you were just following orders, and the planning was all Seldon's, you might get off with life.'

'Life, huh?'

His face was still without expression. I waited for him to say something more, but apparently his conversational mood had passed.

I said, 'Is 'huh' your favorite question?'

He gave me a sardonic grin. 'You got a nice technique, Mr. Moon. If I knew anything about the Lancaster job, I'd probably take the hook. But the night Lancaster stopped a slug I never left my room in Maddon, Illinois, after seven o'clock.'

'Got any witnesses?' I asked.

'You got any that I did?'

I slid off the bed and stuck my hat back on my head. Gesturing to Mike, who had stolidly taken in our whole conversation without a flicker of interest crossing his face, I again started for the door.

Just as I reached it, Percy called, 'Hey, Mr. Moon!'

I looked back over my shoulder.

'Thanks for the cigar,' he said derisively.

12

The rest of that day was as unrewarding as my visit with Percy Sweet, which made it a fairly normal day for leg work. The days you turn up anything new during routine investigation are rare, most of your time being consumed in gathering negative knowledge: that is, by a process of elimination ruling out one possibility after another.

After leaving City Hospital, I made four more calls, none of which added to my knowledge of who killed Walter Lancaster, or why. The first was to headquarters, where I mollified Warren Day by signing formal charges against Percival Sweet and Barney Seldon.

The second was to the Jones and Knight Investment Company, where I learned from Matilda Graves that she had been unable to unearth anything whatever about Willard Knight's personal financial transactions. I found Harlan Jones in, but he seemed as remarkably uninformed about his partner's private affairs as was the secretary-bookkeeper.

My third visit was to Willard Knight's home, where I bullied Mrs. Knight into letting me go through his private papers. And again I drew a blank. If Knight ordinarily kept personal financial records at home, he had removed them along with himself, I decided.

Although from our previous conversation I was reasonably sure Knight did not make a habit of confiding anything at all to his wife, I asked her if she knew what stocks he owned. She didn't. Then I asked her for a picture of her husband, only to learn Lieutenant Hannegan had beat me to the request and the only two photographs she had of him were now at police headquarters.

My fourth visit was back across the river to Carson City, where I spent the rest of the afternoon in the morgue of the Carson City *Herald*. When I finished I had a chronological record of Walter Lancaster's public life, including all the welfare fund drives he had headed during the past twenty years, all the speeches he had made and the community projects he had engaged in, but none of it pointed to anything interesting. If he had ever been involved in anything unsavory, his influence had been great enough to keep it out of the papers.

At six I quit for the day, had a leisurely dinner and went home to shower and dress for my date with Fausta.

When I arrived at the apartment over El Patio, I found Fausta prepared for an evening of riotous gaiety. Her gown, an affair of flaming red which sedately hid her legs clear to the ankles, was not quite so sedate from the waist up. It had no back, no shoulder straps, and so little front she would have been arrested had she appeared in it on a stage. Since obviously it was held up solely by chest expansion, and would embarrass us both the first time she exhaled in public, I balked.

'Some kind of jacket go with that?' I asked tentatively.

'No, I'm all ready.'

'We're not going to a burlesque house,'

I told her. 'Go put some clothes on.'

'Why must you always act like a father when I wear a pretty dress?' she asked irritably. 'Do you think my skin ugly?'

'I've never seen lovelier skin,' I assured her. 'Or so much of it in public. I'm just trying to keep you out of jail.'

'Pooh! You are jealous that other men will look at me.' With her nose in the air she swept out of the apartment and down the stairs.

Since the stairs led down to the same hall where the office was, we had to traverse the whole length of El Patio's dining room to get out of the building. I let her get ten feet ahead of me in the hope people would think I was a casual customer instead of Fausta's escort when we ran the gauntlet, but I could have saved myself the worry. Nobody looked at me anyway. Every eye turned as Fausta passed, however, the male eyes in frank but startled admiration, and the female in outraged envy.

At the front door Mouldy Greene said, 'Hey, that's a pretty rag you got on, Fausta.'

Fausta smiled at him, I pushed open the door, and the ordeal was over.

As I helped her into the car she grinned at me. 'You are such a Puritan, Manny. Most men would drool over my pretty gown, but all you do is look disapproving.'

Rounding the car, I slid under the wheel. 'I like your dress,' I said. 'Particularly the bottom half. But don't come around for sympathy when you get pneumonia.'

'With the temperature eighty-five? Where are we going?'

'I planned on making the rounds. A drink here, a drink there. Maybe a floor show later on. But in that gown I think I'd better take you to the Coal Hole.'

'That dark place?' Fausta asked indignantly. 'I want to go to the Plaza Roof.'

So we went to the Plaza Roof. After that we went to the Jefferson Lounge, the Casino Club, and the Barricades. About eleven thirty we drifted into the Sheridan Hotel.

By then I was used to every eye turning at Fausta when we entered a door, and it no longer bothered me because I realized Fausta's striking beauty covered me with a cloak of invisibility. No doubt everyone who looked at her was aware she was escorted, for had they not been aware of it, every free male in the place would have converged on her the moment she entered; but I don't think anyone's eyes left Fausta's nearly bare torso long enough to note what her escort looked like. My invisibility suited me fine.

The Sheridan's head waiter stopped us just inside the door to inform us in a regretful voice there were no empty tables. He spoke to me, but his eyes remained on Fausta's shoulders.

'We will sit at the bar,' Fausta decided.

At the bar seven men simultaneously vacated their stools for Fausta. Rewarding them all with a sweeping smile, she chose the center one. I decided to stand, and after a moment six of the men reclaimed their seats.

After ordering a rum-and-Coke for Fausta and a rye and water for myself, I turned to look over the house. Almost instantly I spotted George Smith and

Isobel Jones at the same table we had used the previous evening, their heads bent together in such earnest conversation that they were oblivious to everything around them. When neither glanced up, I shrugged and turned back to face the bar.

But as Fausta and I sipped our drinks, periodically I glanced over at Isobel and George. For a long time they remained unconscious of anything but each other. Finally a waiter stopped to clear glasses from their table, and George looked up. His eyes hardened when he saw me, then moved on indifferently and stopped on Fausta. I saw him give a visible start.

He shook his head at the waiter, said something to Isobel and slid from his chair. Casually he moved toward the lobby entrance. At the same time Isobel rose and started toward us, a wide smile of greeting on her face. She said, 'Hello, Manny,' and Fausta swung around on her stool to look her over.

Possibly it was one too many drinks that dulled my reactions, but George was out of sight into the lobby before it registered on me that Isobel had nicely diverted our attention while he made a quiet exit. Remembering his sudden start when he glimpsed Fausta, it looked very much as though the diversion was for her benefit, and George had no desire to be seen by her.

Rapidly I recited, 'Mrs. Jones, Miss Moreni,' then said, 'Pardon me. I see a friend,' and followed quickly after George Smith.

Just inside the lobby I stopped and swept my eyes over the room. George stood diagonally across from me in front of the elevator bank.

A few paces to my right was the bell captain's desk, and Johnny Nelson, the Sheridan's bell captain, stood next to it frowning critically across the room at a bellhop who had allowed his shoulders momentarily to slump a quarter-inch. Once I had unscrambled a case that cleared Johnny of a felony rap, so he owed me a favor. I stepped over to his desk.

'Hello, Mr. Moon,' he said.

I said, 'Quick, Johnny. Take a look at the man by the elevator.'

Johnny glanced toward George just as

the cage doors opened. George stepped in and disappeared to the rear of the car, so that even though the doors remained open as the operator awaited the starter's signal, he was out of our range of vision.

'See him?' I asked.

'Yeah. What about him?'

'He a guest here?'

'Yeah. Came in yesterday morning. Name's Roger Nelson.'

'No,' I said. 'You must have looked at the wrong man. The one I meant is named George Smith.'

'Oh. I thought you meant the guy who got on the elevator. Tall guy with a sloppy haircut.'

'I did. Isn't he George Smith?'

Johnny shook his head emphatically. 'Roger Nelson. Reason I remember, his last name's the same as mine. He's in room fourteen-twelve.'

I thought this over for a minute. 'What else you know about him?'

'Nothing. Never saw him before yesterday.'

'Do me a favor,' I asked. 'See what the desk knows about him.'

'Sure,' said Johnny. 'Wait right here.'

In a few moments he was back. 'It's Neltson, not Nelson,' he informed me. 'Roger Neltson. With a 't.' Registered just before noon yesterday. Home town's Cleveland and firm is Arkwright Type-writers. That's all our check-in form asks. Is he hot?'

'Not that I know. I was just curious.' I slipped him a dollar and returned to the cocktail lounge.

Fausta and Isobel were still at the bar as I had left them, except that Isobel had also managed to acquire a stool. Isobel was nervously watching the door to the lobby, but when I came through it, she turned her face toward the bar in pretended lack of interest.

Fausta looked at me questioningly, and I asked, 'Know a Roger Neltson?'

She looked at me blankly and moved her head in denial.

'Tall, shaggy-haired fellow,' I prompted. 'Looks like Abe Lincoln with a shave. From Cleveland and in the typewriter business.'

She continued to look blank. 'I do not

know such a man.'

Turning my attention to Isobel, I watched her speculatively as she sipped a newly made drink with simulated disregard for our conversation. Feeling my gaze on her, she slid me a glance from eye corners.

'Bourbon and Scotch,' she said, indicating the mixture in her glass. 'I'm completely converted.'

I said to Fausta, 'Pardon us. I want a few private words with Mrs. Jones,' took Isobel firmly by the arm, and led her back to the table she had vacated.

When we were seated across from each other, I glanced back at the bar. Fausta screwed up her nose at me and turned her back.

'All right, Isobel,' I said. 'What's the pitch? Who's Roger Neltson, and why'd you palm him off as George Smith?'

She raised her nose. 'And what business is it of yours who my friends are, or what I choose to call them?'

'None,' I admitted. 'Except when a guy swings at me, I like to know his right name.'

An amused light danced in her eyes for a moment. 'Roger told me about that. Did he really knock you down?'

I stared at her, surprised, then worked up a dry grin. 'I still ache all over. But let's stay on the subject. Why the fake name? And while you were picking one, why didn't you make it John Smith? That's the common alias.'

'None of your business.'

'All right,' I said. 'I'll tell you. He's your extramarital boyfriend and you didn't know he was in town till he walked in here last night. You got all flustered, partly because Mr. Smith-Neltson is the jealous type and partly because you suddenly remembered reading about private cops being blackmailers. So you did a little muddy thinking and sprang the first name that entered your head. How come you didn't give me a fake name too? Something equally original, like Richard Roe?'

She tried to summon forth an offended frown, but her sense of humor got the best of her and she laughed aloud. 'You're a mind-reader. Satisfied now?'

'Did I hit it?'

She nodded sardonically. 'Fairly close, in your blunt, uncouth way. I'm glad my husband hasn't your powers of deduction.' She frowned suddenly and added, 'Or your dirty mind?'

I raised my eyebrows. 'Dirty?'

'You flat-footedly accuse me of having a lover without knowing the first thing about it, really. Mr. Neltson is *not* my extramarital boyfriend, as you call him, but just a friend. I'll have you know — '

' — that you're a respectable married woman,' I finished for her, slightly bored with her belated and illogical virtue. 'Tell me, is Roger jealous of your husband too?'

She raised her nose and got up from her chair. With head high, she swept toward the lobby entrance like a martyred queen. Returning to Fausta at the bar, I stared after Isobel thoughtfully as she disappeared from view.

'From the lady's manner, I would guess you made improper proposals,' Fausta said waspishly.

I ordered another round from the

bartender. A few minutes later Isobel unexpectedly returned. Sliding onto the stool next to Fausta, she held her face expressionless and directed her eyes at the bartender.

'Heard from Knight yet?' I asked her.

For a moment her gaze remained fixedly on the bartender. Then, woodenly, she turned her head at me, said, 'No,' in a definite let-me-alone voice, and returned to her study of the drink mixer.

And at that moment, out of nowhere, something clicked in what I use for a brain. The sudden thought astonished me, not because of its penetration, but because I had been too stupid to see it previously.

'Do you know a Willard Knight?' I asked Fausta.

She frowned thoughtfully. 'Knight,' she repeated. 'Yes, I think so. He is an occasional patron at El Patio. A tall man with shaggy hair.'

Isobel's back stiffened and I grinned at her. 'Right under my nose,' I said. 'I have to see a man, Fausta. Order a drink for Mrs. Jones while I'm gone.'

'Why do you never sit still?' she complained. 'It is certainly lonesome to talk to you, because you go first here, then there, and one is mostly left alone.'

'One can talk to Mrs. Jones until I get back,' I said.

'One can also go with you while you see this man.' She slid from her stool with an air of definiteness about her. Shrugging, I took one bare elbow and piloted her toward the hotel lobby.

At the door I paused to look back. Isobel stared after us, her fists clenched so tightly in her lap the knuckles showed white. The expression on her face was that of a small girl caught in the cookie jar.

When we got on the elevator, Fausta looked at me curiously. But all I said was, 'Fourteen, please.'

When we got off at fourteen, her expression had become speculative. 'When you were gone before, you registered for a room,' she hazarded. 'You think I have drunk too many rum-and-Cokes to know what I am doing?'

'I asked Isobel Jones first,' I growled at her. 'She wasn't drunk enough to give in.'

'Oh, well,' Fausta said philosophically. 'Better second choice than none at all.'

We stopped before 1412, and I raised my fist to knock just as the phone inside began to ring. Dropping my hand, I waited for someone to answer. But the shrill peal went on and on.

Finally, when it was obvious no one was going to answer the phone, I tried the knob. Finding the door unlocked, I pushed it open. A quick glance from the doorway showed no one in the room. The phone, on a stand this side of the bed, continued to ring. Crossing to it, I lifted it from its cradle and said, 'Yes?'

'Willard?' asked Isobel's voice.

'Yes?' I said again.

Her voice was breathless.

'That Moon man knows who you are. I think he's on his way up.'

Fausta had moved from the doorway past the foot of the bed to the windows. Something in her manner caused my gaze to jump at her. She was standing rigid, an expression of shock on her face at something on the floor beyond my range of vision.

In a toneless voice I said into the phone, 'Thanks,' and hung up.

Then, rounding the bed, I stared down at the body of Willard Knight, alias Roger Neltson, alias George Smith.

He lay flat on his back between the bed and the windows, his eyes wide open but sightless. His mouth sagged open too, and the lips had drawn back from his strong teeth to give him an expression of gaping wonder. The whole front of his shirt was soaked with blood from a wound in his chest. His body and the floor immediately around it were sprinkled with feathers. At Knight's feet lay the pillow from which the feathers had come, a powder-blackened hole indicating it had been used by the killer to muffle the sound of the shot.

Taking Fausta by the arm, I led her to the door. 'Wait for me at the bar,' I told her, then pushed her out into the hall and shut the door in her face.

I made a systematic search of the room. A pigskin traveling bag containing a few changes of linen and toilet supplies was all the luggage I found. There were no papers of any sort in it or anywhere else in the room.

Finally I turned to the body. A wallet contained slightly over a hundred dollars in currency, several lodge-membership cards, and a driver's license issued to Willard Knight. His pockets yielded the usual assortment of keys, pocketknife, cigarette lighter and small change, but only one item of any interest.

In his side pants pocket I found a duplicate deposit slip issued by the Riverside Bank, showing a deposit made only that day to the account of the Jones and Knight Investment Company.

The amount shown was seventy thousand dollars.

Putting everything back the way I had found it, I lifted the phone and asked for the house detective.

13

'You had him right in your arms!' Day yelled at me. 'Once you even had him unconscious!' He drew a deep breath. 'So you just stood around until he woke up and took off.'

He was leaning over my chair, his nose approximately an inch from mine so that he could be sure I heard him clearly. Now he straightened, scrubbed a palm over the top of his head in a violent motion which would have left his hair a mess if he had had any, and returned to flop behind his desk. Hannegan, bending above me from the other side, snorted, 'Hah!' and walked over to lean against a wall.

'Can you give me any explanation at all why you didn't report Knight in the first time you saw him?' Day asked in a controlled voice.

'Didn't recognize him,' I said for the twenty-seventh time.

'Oh, stop it!' he snapped. 'You're not that stupid.'

'Yes I am,' I insisted modestly. 'I didn't have a description of Knight and had never seen his picture. I *should* have had, but I muffed it, and I'm not making any excuses. Even without knowing what he looked like, I should have at least wondered if George Smith was Willard Knight, because I had half an idea Mrs. Jones was carrying on an affair with Knight, and George fitted there. But I had Mrs. Jones tagged as a gal who played the field, and assumed she was fooling with *both* Knight and Smith.'

When neither Day nor Hannegan made any reply other than disbelieving scowls, I said, 'I just wasn't awake. I can't be a genius all the time.'

'Hah!' Hannegan snorted again. Two audible statements from the lieutenant within a few minutes was a record, even though both statements consisted of the same word. It led me to believe he was as upset as the inspector.

'If anyone else disappears during this investigation,' I said, 'I'll memorize his description and carry his photograph next to my heart. Why don't you admit what you're really mad about is Knight not being Lancaster's killer, so you could close the case.'

'I never said he was Lancaster's killer!' the inspector half-yelled. 'He was only a suspect.'

'And now who have you got?' I asked. 'A hood who's cagey enough to stay across the river until the heat dies down.'

'Seldon didn't bump Knight,' Day muttered. 'The Illinois cops have been tailing him for me, and he was at a dinner in Madden, Illinois with fifty other people when Knight got it.'

'All his guns got alibis too?' I asked dryly.

The inspector rubbed his head wearily. 'I know Seldon's alibi doesn't mean anything. But Knight's death doesn't necessarily remove Knight as a suspect in the Lancaster killing either. Maybe he bumped Lancaster and the Jones woman bumped him.'

'Oh for cripes' sake!' I said.

'According to you she was gone from

the bar about ten minutes after Knight went upstairs,' he said doggedly. 'She says she went to the ladies' lounge, but she could just as easily have spent the time knocking off her lover.'

'The elevator operator would have remembered taking her up. And don't tell me she walked fourteen flights, shot the guy and walked down again, all in ten minutes.'

'The elevator operator took lots of people up and down last night,' Day growled. 'He wouldn't remember one lone woman.'

'He would a good-looking one like Isobel Jones. Bet you ten bucks if you ask him about Fausta going up with me, he'll remember her.'

'That doesn't prove anything,' the inspector said with such lack of conviction I was sure he had already discovered the elevator boy recalled Fausta. But to myself I had to admit only a dead man would have missed her in that dress.

'Mrs. Jones phoned to tell Knight I was on my way up,' I told him for the umpteenth time. 'She didn't even know he was dead.'

'Could be a cover-up,' he muttered. 'Anyway, we're holding her awhile.'

'What's her husband think?'

Frowning at his ashtray, the inspector began to search for a long butt. 'He thinks we're the Gestapo, apparently. Doesn't believe his wife had a lover. Doesn't believe his partner would have deceived him even if his wife would. If he wasn't so upset, he'd have had a lawyer down here prying her out of jail, but apparently it never occurred to him. He hung around here half the night waiting for somebody to let him see her.'

'Why don't you let him?'

'We will, soon as we get a straight story from Mrs. Jones.' Finding a cigar butt that suited him, the inspector blew it free of ashes and stuffed it in his mouth. 'So far she insists she met Knight accidentally. Claims she went to bed last night the same time as her husband, couldn't sleep, and got up to take a walk. She dropped into the Sheridan simply because it was close to her home, and ran into Knight at the bar. When we jumped her about seeing him there the previous evening when she was with you, she blandly explained she assumed he had just dropped in for a drink, and she didn't realize he was staying there. The reason she gives for introducing him by a fake name is as screwy as the rest of her statement. She says she knew you and the police were hunting Knight, and if she identified him, she'd be called as a witness. Then her husband would discover she'd been out with you instead of home in bed.'

Knowing both the inspector and Hannegan had been up half the night questioning Isobel, I couldn't repress a grin, for I could visualize how her faintly mad manner must have slowly driven them both toward insanity. Day scowled when he saw the grin, and I erased it hurriedly.

'What did you make of the bank-deposit slip in Knight's pocket?' I asked.

For a long time Day glowered at me over his glasses. Then he asked in a soft voice, 'How did you know it was in his pocket? As I recall your statement, you didn't touch the body at all.'

'Just enough to make sure he was

dead,' I said easily. 'You mentioned it yourself. Matter of fact, you almost yelled it.'

He continued to regard me suspiciously, but I could see he wasn't sure. He was so worn out, and had been in so many towering rages during the night, he wasn't sure himself what he had said or not said. He decided to skip it.

'We haven't made anything of it yet. I sent a man over to Riverside Bank when it opened, but he isn't back yet. Jones didn't know what it meant either. I sprang it on him about nine this morning and he nearly had a conniption fit. He took off in the direction of the bank like a scared rabbit.'

The phone rang at that moment and the inspector answered it. 'Day,' he said, then grunted twice and hung up.

'Ballistics,' he offered in a discouraged voice. 'The slug hit a bone and was all mashed up, just like in the Lancaster killing. All they can give me is it was a thirty-eight. And since there was no casing found in the room, probably a revolver was used.'

'Unless the murderer stopped to pick up the ejected cartridge.'

'Yeah,' Day said. 'So it might be the same gun used on Lancaster, or it might not. What I like about this case is all the scientific help we get from our hundred-thousand-dollar laboratory.'

'Speaking of the laboratory, did you give Isobel Jones a paraffin test?'

Over by the wall Hannegan emitted a snort.

The inspector said, 'We stopped using it.'

'Huh?' I asked in surprise.

'You're behind the times,' Day said irritably. 'We stopped taking paraffin impressions six months ago. What's the use, when they're no good in court?'

'I didn't know they were no good.'

'Well, you know now. Light a cigarette with a kitchen match and the paraffin test will prove you fired a gun even if you never had one in your hand. Get a little inaccurate in the bathroom, forget to wash your hands, and the same thing. Urine gives the nicest positive reaction you'd ever want to see.' Reaching under his coat, he produced his short-barreled Detective-Special. 'On the other hand, you can fire a good tight gun like this all day long, and the paraffin test will prove you never touched it because there's no flashback.'

'Well,' I said. 'You learn something every day.'

Putting the gun away, Day said, 'And take fingerprints. Every time somebody gets killed, the public wants to know about fingerprints. Know how many usable fingerprints we found in Knight's hotel room?'

I admitted I didn't.

'One. Exactly one. On the underside of the dresser's glass top. Probably belongs to the guy who set the top there when the room was furnished. Every other print in the room was so smudged it was useless for comparison. Look here.' Pulling a glass paperweight before him, the inspector rubbed it clean with his handkerchief. 'Now there's a perfect surface for fingerprints, wouldn't you say?'

'You'd think so,' I agreed.

Gently he placed an index finger

against the glass.

'If I touch it lightly like this, I leave a nice print. But if I press too hard' — he illustrated by increasing the pressure — 'the print smudges. Fingerprints are wonderful for identification purposes, but I never yet solved a murder by finding fingerprints on anything.'

Picking up the paperweight, he tossed it from one hand to the other a half-dozen times, then shoved it toward me. 'Take that up to the fingerprint bureau, and I'll bet you ten bucks they don't bring out a single print good enough for comparison purposes.'

Knowing Warren Day's eagerness to part with money was approximately equal to my eagerness to part with another leg, I declined the bet. 'I'll take your word for it, Inspector. I'm convinced that scientific criminal investigation, television, and the horseless carriage are all flops. The blacksmith, vaudeville, and homicide cops who can't read will have their day yet.'

'Oh, the hell with you, Moon! I try to educate you a little and you crack wise.'

A knock sounded at the door. Day

growled, 'Yes?' and a uniformed cop entered.

'Fellow named Robert Caxton asking to see you, Inspector.'

'Caxton?' Day repeated. 'Oh, that taxi driver in the Lancaster case. What's he want?'

'Wouldn't say, sir. Wants to talk to you.'

'All right,' the inspector said impatiently. 'Send him in. You can go, Moon, but keep in touch with me.'

The cop backed out, but I made no effort to move.

'We're sharing all information, remember, Inspector? I'll stick around to see what Caxton wants.'

The inspector scowled at me, but decided to let it ride. A moment later the little taxi driver came in, scowled at me also, then turned his attention to Warren Day.

'I figured I better bring this straight to you, Inspector. I got to thinking about this phone call I got yesterday morning, and the more I thought about it, the screwier it seemed.'

'What call was that?'

180

'From this guy who said he was a reporter for the *Morning Blade*. Got me out of bed about nine yesterday morning. Usually I don't get up till noon, see, because I work the four-till-midnight shift. I was half-dopey with sleep, or I might have tumbled something was fishy at the time, but I never thought about it until this morning when the phone got me out of bed again and some woman asked what radio program I was listening to. Then when I got to thinking about this reporter's call, I dressed and came right over.'

'Well, get to it,' the inspector said impatiently. 'What'd he want?'

'Just getting background for a human-interest story on the Lancaster case, he said. Wanted some dope about the witnesses. Asked how long I'd run a cab, whether I was married or not. That kind of stuff. When he was finished asking about me, he said kind of casual-like, 'Let's see, you're the third witness I've called. Thomas Henning — that's the doorman; Manville Moon, the customer who saw it; and you. What was the name of that fourth witness again?' Being half-asleep, I said, 'You mean Miss Moreni, the lady who runs El Patio?' and he said, 'That's it. Forgot the name for a minute.' Then he thanked me and hung up.'

All three of us were glaring at him by the time he finished. Day and Hannegan continued to look at him, but I swung my glare at the inspector.

'So you put tails on the witnesses,' I said bitterly. 'If the killer approached either of them, all you had to do was grab him. But being so scientific-minded, it never occurred to you he might make use of a modern invention like the telephone.'

Day swung at me. 'It never occurred to you either. You knew what the setup was.'

Not deigning to answer, I jerked his desk phone from its cradle and gave the police switchboard Fausta's apartment number. When it had rung for three minutes without answer, I hung up and tried the bar phone downstairs. Since it was only ten a.m. and El Patio did not open till noon, I was not surprised that it took another three minutes before I got an answer there. The voice that finally answered sounded like it belonged to a porter.

'Fausta around?' I asked.

'No, suh.'

'Is Mouldy Greene there?'

'Back in his room, maybe. Want I should look?'

'Get him to the phone fast,' I snapped. 'Got that? I want him right now.'

'Yes, suh,' he said in a startled voice, and I heard him drop the receiver on the bar.

Another two minutes passed before Mouldy's belligerent voice said, 'Who's in such a rush?'

'Moon,' I said. 'Where's Fausta?'

'Oh, hello, Sarge.' His voice turned friendly. 'Ain't she showed up yet?'

I felt my stomach turn over. 'Showed up where?'

'Wherever you was supposed to meet her.'

'Look, Mouldy,' I said desperately, 'try to get this the first time I say it. I wasn't supposed to meet Fausta anywhere. The guy who killed Lancaster knows she was the fourth witness, and if a fake call came for her, it was from him.'

'Huh?'

'For cripes' sake, get your brains together, Mouldy. A killer may have hold of Fausta.'

'A killer? Just a minute, Sarge.' There was a dull clunk as the phone was laid on the bar.

'Mouldy!' I said. When there was no answer, I yelled, 'Mouldy, you goddamned idiot!'

There was still no answer, and I sat there with the phone glued to my ear a full two minutes, glaring from the inspector to Hannegan to Caxton and then starting the circuit over again. I was almost ready to hang up and start driving toward El Patio when Mouldy returned. And by then I was so mad I couldn't speak.

'Hadda talk to Romulus a minute,' he said calmly. 'He's the porter who answered the phone. About an hour ago the bar phone rang and Romulus answered. Some guy said he was you and he'd been trying to get Fausta's apartment, but something was wrong with her phone. Then he told

Romulus to tell Fausta to meet you at the Sheridan Cocktail Lounge at ten o'clock. She called a taxi and left here at nine thirty.'

14

I was too amazed by Mouldy's unexpected coherence to speak for a moment.

In the same calm voice he said, 'I guess you'll want to do it, but if this guy bumps Fausta, I get to kill him, Sarge. Okay?'

When I was able to speak I choked out, 'Okay.'

'Meet you at the Sheridan,' he said, and hung up.

As I started for the door Warren Day said, 'Wait a minute, Moon. What happened?'

I stopped with my hand on the knob. Over my shoulder I said, 'Your killer used my name as a lure, and Fausta may be dead by now. If you want to help rectify the results of your clever trap, start phoning cab companies to find out who made a trip from El Patio to the Sheridan at nine thirty.' Pulling open the door, I passed through and slammed it behind me without waiting for a reply.

In the time it took me to cross the street and climb into my Plymouth, Warren Day must have started a couple of plain-clothes men on my tail, for as I pulled away I noticed a blue sedan swing into a U-turn from in front of headquarters and fall in behind me. I had not seen the men come out of the building — as a matter of fact had not even noticed the blue sedan as I rushed past it — but in my rear-view mirror I could see the car contained two men and there was no doubt in my mind it was a tail.

I decided to give them a ride for their money. The Sheridan is a good four miles from headquarters, most of the distance requiring travel through the city's most congested district. Nevertheless I made it in five minutes flat, leaving a stream of curses in my wake and at least two traffic cops with apoplexy. I was too busy driving to check whether or not the blue sedan was able to stay with me, but apparently the driver was an expert, for as I slowed down just short of the Sheridan, it pulled next to me and the man next to the driver waved me over to the curb.

Surprisingly, I had passed not a single radio car or motor cop during my entire trip, so the blue sedan had been alone in its chase. I could hear sirens begin to drone in the distance, however, which led me to believe at least one of the traffic cops I had emotionally upset had gotten to a phone.

Figuring I would be unable to find a parking spot closer to the Sheridan's front door anyway, I pulled into a loading zone just across the street from the hotel and climbed out of the car. The blue sedan double-parked next to me and emitted its spare passenger at the same moment.

The sedan bore nothing to identify it as a police car, but the man who got out immediately flashed a badge. He was a middle-aged heavy-set man with a bull neck and a face nearly as flat as Mouldy Greene's.

'If Inspector Day set you on my tail, he didn't tell you to get in my hair,' I snapped at him. 'Check with Day later, if you want, but don't try to stop me now.'

One or two passers-by had stopped to gape at us curiously. The bull-necked man paid no attention to them, but held his coat wide so they could not fail to see his badge, and suddenly drew a short-barreled gun with his other hand. 'Get in the back, buster,' he ordered.

'Now wait a minute,' I said. 'I'm on my way to prevent a murder witness from getting killed. Come along if you want, but if you delay me, Warren Day will have your scalp.'

There was a click as the hammer of the short-barreled gun drew back. And a sudden thinness about the man's lips warned me he would have no compunction about squeezing the trigger.

A *trigger-happy cop*, I thought with a sense of shock. *The guy wants an excuse to shoot somebody.*

Opening the sedan's rear door, I got in the back. As the heavy-set man climbed in next to me, still holding me under his gun, I said, 'Don't blame me if you end up walking a beat.'

'All right, Slim,' my arrester said to the thin-faced man behind the wheel, and the sedan moved away with a purr of power.

It was not till then that I got it. 'Oh,' I

said, glancing down at the cocked gun. 'I forgot you could buy tin badges in a dime store.'

'You catch on fast, buster. Just hold still now.' His left hand reached across and patted me beneath the arms and at the waist. 'No artillery, huh?'

'I didn't realize anybody was gunning for me,' I apologized. 'I'll start wearing some tomorrow. What did you do with Fausta?'

The heavy-set man looked me over thoughtfully. Finally he asked, 'Miss Moreni?'

'You been setting traps for any other women named Fausta?'

We were rolling sedately along in the direction of Midland Park. The car stopped for a red light at Mason Avenue, and my rear-seat companion continued to regard me thoughtfully.

'Something happen to Miss Moreni?' The way he asked it made me think he actually didn't know. There was a note of doubtfulness in his voice, and had it not been for the cocked gun pointing unwaveringly at my stomach, I might have gotten the impression he was upset at the thought of anything happening to Fausta.

As the car moved forward again, he said, 'Speak up, buster. What gives with Miss Moreni?'

It was my turn to regard him thoughtfully. 'You really don't know?'

'Buster, we sat in front of your apartment house since six a.m., and we'd have grabbed you when you came out at eight if Slim hadn't gone to sleep when he was supposed to be watching.' The driver interspersed an irritated grunt. 'By the time he woke up, you were pulling out of the garage and there was nothing we could do but tail you. Ever since, we been parked across from police headquarters. We don't know from nothing about Miss Moreni.'

Wryly I thought that if Warren Day's early-morning call had not gotten me out of bed four hours prior to my usual rising time, I might still be peacefully sleeping at home instead of being taken for a ride by a couple of hoods. Then I also had to admit to myself I wouldn't have known about Fausta's danger. Not that knowing about it seemed to be doing me any good.

I asked, 'Why are you interested?'

His expression grew irked. 'I'm going to ask once more, buster, then put a slug in your guts. What's with Miss Moreni?'

It did not seem to me that suppressing the story was worth a slug in the guts, for though I completely failed to understand his interest in Fausta, I couldn't see how his knowing about the fake call she had received would put her in any more danger than she already was in. So I told him.

By now we were driving through Midland Park, presumably in search of a quiet spot where they could dump my body, or give me a going-over, or do whatever else they had in mind. My stocky seatmate surprised me by suddenly ordering the driver to turn around.

Nosing onto a bridle path, Slim expertly backed the car and headed it back the way it had come.

'Hold it,' the heavy-set gunman said before the car started forward motion again. Then to me, 'All right, buster. Out you go.'

I looked at him without understanding, but when he waggled his short-nosed revolver at me, I opened the door on my side and climbed out.

'Push it shut again.'

Pushing it shut, I stared at him through the window.

'Keep your nose clean, buster.' As the car shot forward, I heard him say, 'Back to the Sheridan. And don't spare the horses.'

They had left me approximately a mile inside the park on the road going past the art museum. However, ten thirty a.m. apparently was not a good hour for art lovers, for not a person or a car was in sight in any direction. I started to walk.

I am sufficiently used to an artificial leg so that it is rarely a handicap any more, but I will never become an expert hiker. Walking as fast as I could, it took me fifteen minutes to get to the edge of the park. And then, of course, there was no cab in sight.

Directly across from the park's main entrance on Park Lane was a huge cut-rate drugstore. The sidewalk in front of the store also happened to be an express bus stop, and I mentally tossed a coin to decide whether to use one of the drugstore's phones to call a cab, or take a chance on a bus coming along within the next few minutes. The expresses only ran every twenty minutes.

Inside my head the coin came down tails for the bus. One stopped five minutes later.

When I got off the bus across the street from the Sheridan, my watch told me it was exactly thirty-two minutes since my heavy-set friend had abandoned me in the park. I saw no sign of the blue sedan, but my Plymouth stood where I had left it in the loading zone, unchanged except for a bright pink ticket attached to the windshield wiper. Somehow it failed to amuse me to discover the police were still diligently on the job ticketing parking violations while Fausta possibly was in the hands of a killer.

A crowd was gathered on the sidewalk outside the Sheridan, and a uniformed cop tried to stop me from entering the lounge. 'Sorry, sir,' he said in the mechanical manner of one who has been repeating the same phrase over and over. 'There's been an accident and the bar is closed.'

Just beyond the cop I saw the straw-hatted figure of Warren Day, an unlighted cigar in his mouth thrust upward at an angle as he peered down sourly at a sheet-covered figure lying on the floor. I was conscious of a number of other people wandering around the barroom, but Day was the only one I really saw before my eyes touched the motionless figure, and after that I couldn't even see him.

I said, 'I'm with Inspector Day,' and when the cop didn't move aside at once, put my hand against his chest and pushed.

'Hey!' he said, staggering back.

'Take it up with the inspector,' I snarled at him, strode over to the sheet-covered figure and glared down at it. The inspector watched silently as I fell to one knee and tenderly lifted an edge of the cloth.

The body beneath the sheet was as a dead as a body can get. Lips were drawn back in a grimace of agony, and the face had a faintly bluish cast.

But it was not Fausta. It was a man I had never in my life seen before.

Dropping the sheet, I slowly rose and looked at Warren Day. He simply looked back at me, not even scowling for a change. Then he jerked his head sideways at a corner of the room.

Turning, I saw one of the most welcome sights I have ever seen. Seated at a table with her back to me, calmly smoking a cigarette, was Fausta, and hovering over her in the belligerent manner of a mastiff guarding a bone was Mouldy Greene.

A half-dozen quick steps took me to the table. Sinking my fingers in her blonde hair, I jerked back her head, leaned over and planted a solid kiss on her lips.

'That's for nothing,' I growled at her. 'Scare me like this again and I'll beat hell out of you.'

She looked up at me from round eyes, for once startled into quietness. Then she touched her lips where mine had bruised them and a wicked expression grew on her face. 'You kissed me,' she said. 'In front of witnesses. Mouldy, did you see?'

'Yeah, I saw. Where you been, Sarge?'

'Later,' I said. Rounding the table, I sat across from Fausta. 'Let's have the story,

Fausta. All of it, including who the dead man is.'

Warren Day pulled out a chair and wearily sat down also. His face was so drawn with fatigue, he looked as though he just made it before he collapsed to the floor.

'Yeah,' he said. 'Let's have it. All I've been able to figure out so far is the dead guy is one of the waiters.'

15

Fausta's story was brief and not very enlightening. In response to my supposed request, she had arrived at the Sheridan just before ten, dismissed her cab, and asked the head waiter for me. He informed her that Mr. Moon had phoned he would be a few minutes late and left instructions for her to take a table for both of them. At ten in the morning a table was no problem, for the cocktail lounge was built to accommodate two hundred, there were less than thirty customers in the place, and half of these were at the bar. Fausta chose the corner table where we were sitting now.

A few minutes later she was quietly smoking a cigarette while she waited, when a waiter set in front of her what seemed to be a rum-and-Coke, then moved off to another table before she could speak. She looked at it in surprise, then simply let it stand there until she was able to attract the waiter's attention.

When she finally managed to signal him over, she said, 'You have made a mistake. I ordered no drink.'

'It's on the gentleman at the bar,' he said. 'Mr. Moon.' He turned to point out Mr. Moon, failed to find him and said, 'He must have stepped to the men's room.'

Still more puzzled than annoyed, Fausta sniffed the drink, detected the odor of rum, and instructed the waiter to take it away and bring her a plain Coke. While she was not in the least suspicious, and assumed I had actually sent over the drink, then disappeared into the washroom and would be along in a minute, the murderer's simple plot was foiled by his lack of knowledge of Fausta.

Fausta never touched anything alcoholic before one in the afternoon.

The waiter removed the rum-and-Coke, but apparently decided not to toss it down the drain. Since it had been paid for, he took it into the liquor storeroom and tossed it down himself.

Fausta, of course, did not know this at

the time. Her story ended with the waiter taking away the drink. When customers at the bar set up an excited clamoring a few minutes later, she had no idea what had caused it. She did learn from the general conversation that someone had been found dead in the storeroom, apparently of a heart attack, but did not connect it with her rejected drink, or for that matter did not even know the dead man was her waiter until after the police arrived.

'We got here fast,' Day said to me wearily. 'We were already on our way because of what you said when you tore out of my office. The guy hadn't been dead five minutes, and the management hadn't even gotten around to calling us when we took the joint by storm. We weren't in time to prevent half the customers from taking a powder the minute they smelled murder though. The poisoner with them, most likely.'

'It was poison, was it?' I asked.

'The medic hazards a guess at potassium cyanide, though he can't say for sure until after an autopsy. He thinks he got a faint whiff of bitter almonds, though rum-and-Coke is a pretty good cover for the smell. The taste too, for that matter. The symptoms are hard to tell from an ordinary heart attack: instant death, cyanosis. If we hadn't rolled in looking for murder, it probably would have passed as a heart attack.'

He scratched his long nose and burst out irritably, 'The stuff is too easy to buy. Farmers use tons of it to kill pests. Sign your name and you can get enough in any drugstore to kill a regiment. Sign a fake name, and unless the druggist recalls your description, you're a successful murderer. Half my men will be tied up the next week checking drugstores.'

Fausta's narrow escape had not increased my present regard for the inspector. I said without sympathy, 'For a week they'll be earning their salaries anyway.'

Day glared at me.

'What's the bartender say?' I asked. 'Maybe he remembers who ordered Fausta's rum-and-Coke.'

It developed Day had not yet questioned the bartender, or anyone else either. He had been in the place only about twenty minutes before I arrived, and only a minute or two before I walked in had gotten the medical examiner's opinion that it might be a cyanide death.

He called Hannegan over from the other side of the room and told him to bring over the bartender.

The barkeep was a sad-faced man in his late fifties who had looked across the bar at so much human idiocy during his lifetime, nothing could upset him very much, including murder. He had no idea who had ordered the rum-and-Coke. Vaguely he recalled mixing one a short time before the waiter's death, but being alone behind the bar, and with over a dozen customers plus two waiters to take care of, he could not remember to whom he gave it.

'I never look at their faces anyway unless they make conversation,' he said sadly. 'I think it was one of the customers instead of a waiter, but I'm not even sure of that.'

The dead waiter's name was Harold Rosenthal, and he was forty-four years old and a bachelor, the bartender informed us. As far as he knew, the man had no living relatives. The surviving waiter knew even less. In fact he knew nothing at all. Nor did any of the approximately one dozen remaining customers who had not been smart enough to scoot off before the police arrived. No one at all recalled even seeing the bartender mix a rum-and-Coke, let alone remembering who had received it.

The head waiter was a little help. The phone call from 'Mr. Moon' had come to the bar phone, and he had taken it. The voice had not impressed him as particularly distinctive, either high or low, soft or harsh, but he felt he could identify it if he heard it again. Why he felt he could, he did not say, and the inspector did not press him. My own opinion was it gave him a feeling of importance to be a witness, and he could no more identify the voice if he heard it again than he could do a hula on a tightrope.

I suggested to Day that since the murderer had appeared on the scene almost immediately after the phone call, he had probably called from one of the pay phones in the lobby of the hotel. He agreed with me, but this put us no closer to a solution.

On the basis of what confused information was available, we came to the conclusion the killer had probably watched the lounge from the lobby entrance, and as soon as he saw Fausta seat herself, had approached the bar and ordered the rum-and-Coke as though intending to drink it himself. Then he must have slipped in the cyanide, handed the glass to the waiter, and told him it was for Fausta with the compliments of Mr. Moon. By the time the drink was delivered, he could have disappeared again through the lobby entrance.

'The invisible man!' the inspector grated disgustedly. 'Commits a murder in front of thirty people and nobody even sees him!'

'We know one thing about him anyway,' I offered.

He stared at me. 'What?'

'He was well enough acquainted with Fausta to know her favorite drink is rum-and-Coke, but not well enough to know she never drinks in the morning.'

Day's expression turned disgusted. 'That narrows it down to the fifty-thousand people who have stopped at El Patio sometime or other and may have seen her order a drink at the bar.'

'I was thinking of Barney Seldon,' I said. 'The only time he ever sees her is in the evening.'

Fausta said, 'Barney Seldon is a love in my life. He would not hurt a hair of my head.'

'He'd rub you out without batting an eye if he thought you were a witness against him,' I said brutally. 'Get it in your head your pretty boyfriend is a hood.'

'A jerk too,' Mouldy offered brightly. 'Hey, Fausta?'

Fausta did not even look at him.

'There must have been some reason the Sheridan was picked,' I said thoughtfully. 'The killer would want to make the meeting place somewhere plausible so that Fausta wouldn't question it, and she might have if a bar had been picked neither of us ever went to. We know the killer was here last night when we were, because he killed Knight. Possibly he saw us then, and assumed it was a regular hangout of ours.'

'Your friend Isobel Jones was here last night,' Fausta put in. 'Also she sat next to me at the bar and saw I drank rum-and-Coke.'

I looked at her. 'This was a man. Isobel could hardly pass herself off as somebody named Mr. Moon. Anyway, she's in jail.'

'Maybe she has an accomplice.'

'If she has, she couldn't have passed along the information that you like rum-and-Cokes,' I said. 'She's been in jail ever since last night.'

'Go ahead,' Fausta said unreasonably. 'Defend her just because you have the mistaken idea she is beautiful.'

I changed the subject by telling Warren Day about the blue sedan and my heavy-set, flat-faced abductor.

'So that's where you were,' he commented. 'Riding in the park while I rushed to the rescue of your girlfriend.'

I forbore reminding him Fausta's drinking habits had saved her, and not the inspector's rushing, as he would have been about ten minutes late had she accepted the drink. 'I don't pretend to understand it,' I said. 'But the news about Fausta being in a killer's trap changed the guy's mind about me entirely. All of a sudden he just seemed to lose interest and took off for the Sheridan.'

'Nobody with a flat face turned up here,' the inspector said. He looked at Mouldy Greene. 'Nobody I didn't know, anyway.'

Fausta said, 'I do not know anyone of that description.'

'Me neither,' Mouldy injected. 'A guy as ugly as you describe, you'd be bound to remember him.'

Beyond taking down the names of the remaining customers and questioning hotel employees in the lobby in an effort to discover if anyone had noticed a man hanging around the entrance to the cocktail lounge, which none did, there was nothing more Day could do at the moment. I went off with Fausta and Mouldy, leaving the inspector staring dourly at the sheet-covered corpse.

It was not until we were nearly to my

Plymouth that I remembered my parking ticket. Mouldy held open the car door for Fausta, but instead of climbing in the driver's side, I slipped the ticket from under the windshield wiper, said I would be right back, and returned to the Sheridan Lounge. Thrusting the pink card at Warren Day, I said, 'I got this when my gun-happy abductor forced me over to the curb into a loading zone.'

Day regarded it without interest. 'I'm not in the Traffic Division, Moon.'

'I was on Homicide business at the time.'

'Not officially, you weren't. It's not my responsibility if you go tearing after killers on your own.'

'All right,' I said, withdrawing the ticket. 'But I'm not going in to pay the fine. I'll go to police court and explain right out loud why I parked in the zone. Because I was in a hurry to prevent Inspector Warren Day's killer trap from snapping on the wrong person. The papers love little human-interest stories like that.'

He was so tired from being up all night, he didn't even bother to scowl at me.

'Give me the damn thing,' he said wearily.

Even though my car was parked across the side street edging the hotel, a full quarter block from the lounge entrance, the moment I stepped out on the sidewalk I spotted another pink ticket under the windshield wiper. My hat nearly rose off my head in rage, and I literally ran to the loading zone.

It was not until I had reached across the hood and jerked loose the pink slip that I realized it was paper instead of cardboard. Examining it, I discovered it was not a parking ticket at all; it was only an out-of-date bus transfer.

I glanced through the windshield at Fausta and Mouldy. Fausta's face was perfectly expressionless, but Mouldy was slapping his leg in a convulsion of glee.

16

I did not run Fausta and Mouldy back to El Patio immediately. It was noon when we got away from the Sheridan, and the three of us stopped for lunch at a Johnson's restaurant a few blocks beyond the Sheridan.

During lunch I firmly instructed Fausta concerning her immediate future. 'You're not playing hostess at El Patio until this killer is laid by the heels,' I told her. 'Wandering around among two hundred diners every night, any one of which might be the killer, would be sticking your head on the block. You've got two choices. You may go to jail for protection, or have me move in as a bodyguard.'

'Move in?' she asked interestedly. 'In my apartment?'

'Strictly as a business arrangement. The daybed in your front room will suit fine. But I want you to understand ahead of time, it's going to be up to you to arrange your life to suit mine. I'm on this case and I can't drop it in order to follow you around. You're going to have to follow me. Every day, all day long, until I tuck you in at night. You'll have to forget managing El Patio.'

'I can run the joint,' Mouldy said.

Fausta looked at him. 'It will run itself for a few days,' she said firmly. 'You just stick to your regular job.'

'Then you agree to those terms?' I asked.

'It will be interesting to have you around twenty-four hours a day like an unemployed husband. Maybe I will become bored with you and begin to appreciate Barney Seldon more.'

After lunch I drove over to my apartment, packed a weekend bag and strapped my P-38 under my arm. Then the three of us rode out to El Patio and I moved into my new home.

As soon as we arrived, Fausta had to make a tour of the place to inform her various employees they would be on their own for the immediate future. Mouldy took over my job of bodyguarding to conduct her on the tour while I unpacked my small bag, found some sheets in Fausta's linen cabinet, and made up the daybed in the front room.

I had just finished when Fausta came in alone. She looked at the made-up daybed in surprise. 'This is not going to be very comfortable,' she said, poking at it tentatively.

'It'll do. I probably won't spend much time in it anyway.'

'No?' she asked, elevating her brows.

'Work to do,' I explained. 'Can't spend all my time in bed.'

She frowned at me. 'You are an exasperating person, Manny Moon. With any man but you in the front room, I would move a chaperone into my bedroom. But with you I know I am safe.'

Walking into her own room, she slammed the door. Almost immediately it opened again and she said distinctly, 'I would not let you in my bedroom if you begged on hands and knees, but you do not have to make a girl feel so goddamned safe!' The door slammed again. It was the first time I had ever heard Fausta swear.

I waited a few minutes, then knocked on the door. When nothing happened, I opened it and peered in. Fausta was seated on the bed smoking a cigarette.

'The following starts now,' I said. 'I'm off to headquarters, so stop sulking and come along.'

'I do not think I want to follow you around.'

'You don't have any choice,' I told her. 'Either follow willingly, or I'll haul you down and have Day slap you in protective custody as a material witness.'

Her eyes glittered at me, but she made no move.

Walking over to the bed, I took the cigarette from her hand, crushed it out on a bedstand ashtray and jerked her to her feet. Grabbing her by the shoulders, I slammed her against my chest and kissed her.

One sharp-toed pump kicked against my good leg. Momentarily she writhed like a snake and tried to turn her head away, then suddenly wound her arms about my neck and started to choke me to death. All at once instead of kissing her, I found myself simply hanging on while she kissed me. Just as steam began to issue from my ears, she jerked free, stepped back a pace and regarded me with her head cocked to one side.

I reached for her again, but she side-stepped with a mocking smile and calmly walked into the front room. In the glass over the mantel she repaired her lipstick while I watched broodingly. I realized my reaching for her after she had jerked away had been a mistake, for all she had wanted was a show of interest on my part so that she could repulse it. I had reacted exactly as she wanted, and for the rest of the day she would probably treat me with standoffish skittishness, as though I were a wolf whose passes she must constantly guard against. I contemplated the prospect dubiously, recognizing she had neatly managed to reverse our usual roles.

Wiping the lipstick from my mouth with a handkerchief, I growled at her, 'If the temperament fit is over, let's go.'

At police headquarters we were informed both Warren Day and Lieutenant

Hannegan were taking naps in the infirmary and had left instructions for no one to rouse them until four. Since it was only two p.m. when we arrived, I told the desk we wouldn't wait. As an afterthought I inquired about Isobel Jones, and learned she had been released on bond as a material witness only an hour before.

'Let's visit the lady's husband,' I said to Fausta. 'Probably I can get the same information from him I wanted from the inspector anyway.'

In the outer office of the Jones and Knight Investment Company we found the secretary-bookkeeper Matilda Graves poring over a huge ledger. As nearly as I could tell the ledger contained nothing but columns of figures, but they must have been sad figures, for she furtively dabbed at her eyes with a piece of Kleenex when we entered, and her face was flushed from weeping. Surely Knight's death had not brought on her grief, I thought, for during our previous conversations I had gotten the distinct impression she not only did not care much for the shaggy-haired partner, but was actually afraid of him.

Later, during our conversation with her remaining employer, we learned Matilda's tears were solely for herself, and stemmed from Jones's discovery that she had been doing a sloppy job of bookkeeping.

When she spoke to Harlan Jones over the intercom, she announced only that I was there, so Fausta entering his private office with me was a surprise to him. We found him feverishly comparing a pile of bank statements with what seemed to be a stack of duplicate deposit slips. He did not seem particularly glad to see me, but his eyes lighted with almost breathless interest when they touched Fausta.

'Miss Fausta Moreni,' I said. 'This is Mr. Jones, Fausta.'

Jones's round body popped out of its chair like a bounced rubber ball. His face fixed in an almost groveling smile, he told Fausta he was delighted to meet her and quickly rounded the desk to hold a chair for her. He let me find my own chair.

When he had fussily reseated himself, he continued to gaze at Fausta as though fascinated. It was a common reaction for men to pant slightly the first time they saw Fausta, but Jones seemed to be overdoing it. I glanced at her to check if our momentary struggle at her apartment had loosened some strap and allowed more of her to show than she intended, but she was as fully dressed as is customary for women to dress during the summer in our part of the country. That is not very fully, but Fausta's lightweight sleeveless dress exposed nothing more interesting than her smooth shoulders and equally smooth neck.

I finally deduced Harlan Jones was not upset so much by Fausta as just plain upset. The emotion he was exhibiting was not passion, but ordinary nervousness, and I guessed that our appearance had nothing to do with it. He had been jittering like a monkey on a string before we ever entered the office, I decided; and since he was poring over bank statements when we arrived, I guessed it was these which had raised his blood pressure.

I said, 'I understand Mrs. Jones was released finally, Mr. Jones.'

'Yes,' he said, wrenching his nervous gaze from Fausta long enough to look at me. 'I just spoke to her on the phone. She plans to take a shower and then nap until she recovers from the ordeal.'

The ordeal had been two-sided, I thought. She had accounted for herself pretty well inasmuch as she had Homicide's two top men laid out on their backs.

'What I really dropped in about was the bank-deposit slip found in Willard Knight's pocket,' I said. 'Inspector Day told me you went to the bank this morning to check on it. Find out anything?'

'I'm still finding things out,' he said, gesturing toward the pile of bank statements and deposit slips on his desk. 'It's a rather appalling discovery to make about a dead partner, but it seems Knight has been juggling the basic company account for some time.'

'Finding shortages?'

He shook his head. 'Fortunately no. At least as nearly as I can make out from a quick check, and I don't believe that an audit will disclose any shortage either. But had it not been for the deposit Knight made only yesterday afternoon just a few hours before he died, the firm would be seventy thousand short. And that would have meant bankruptcy.' Drawing a handkerchief from his pocket, he wiped the back of his neck and shivered again over the narrow escape.

'The seventy thousand belonged to the firm, did it?' I asked. 'And Knight replaced it on the q.t.?'

'Worse than that. It was a client's money in our custody. Apparently Knight had been using funds entrusted to us for his own personal speculations for nearly a year. Frequently instead of depositing a check received from a client, he would use the money for market speculation first, then deposit it after he had made use of it. Apparently he was consistently lucky, or at least not unlucky, for while I am sure he never made any very substantial profits, he never seems to have lost his illegally borrowed capital either. At least the records indicate he always managed to deposit what he had withheld before the last day of the month, so that the bank statement always showed the proper balance.'

'He never held out deposits more than thirty days then?'

'No,' Jones said. 'Sometimes for periods only as long as two or three days. I imagine he would buy some shares, wait for a rise above his purchase price, then immediately sell out, pocket whatever profit he had made and deposit the capital he had withheld.'

'But wouldn't your bookkeeper catch the discrepancies between the dates amounts were supposed to be deposited and the actual dates of deposit?'

Harlan Jones's angry flush told me what had caused Matilda Graves tears. 'She should have, but Knight seemingly knew her shortcomings better than I did. Miss Graves is an efficient secretary and bookkeeper, but apparently she doesn't do any unnecessary work. The way my partner worked, it was really quite simple. By mutual agreement he always took care of bank deposits — that is, he made all trips to the bank. Miss Graves prepared the deposit slips. The account he was tampering with is the company's basic checking account, into which all monies received are always deposited. We have three other accounts: a petty cash fund of five hundred dollars which Miss Graves is authorized to write checks against for rent, utilities and so forth; a savings account in our joint names; and an expense account both Knight and I were authorized to write checks against. But deposits to these accounts are always by transfer of funds from the basic account, you see, and never by direct deposit of monies received. In this way *all* money transactions have to pass through the basic account, which simplifies bookkeeping.'

When I believed I had this absorbed, I said, 'For instance, your firm receives a profit of a thousand dollars from some transaction, and you decide to deposit it in your savings account. Instead of making a direct deposit, you stick it in the basic account, then write a check against the basic account for one thousand dollars and deposit that.'

'Exactly. So all Miss Graves's book entries represent either a deposit or a check written against the basic account.

Apparently Willard figured that as long as the final figure on the bank statement jibed with the balance in Miss Graves's books when she totaled up at the end of each month, she wouldn't bother to check the deposits appearing on the bank statement against her file of deposit slips. What Willard did was have a rubber stamp made similar to the one the bank uses on duplicate deposit slips. I found it in his desk this morning.'

Fumbling in his desk drawer, he produced a large rubber stamp, held it up for a moment and dropped it back in the drawer again. 'Instead of using a bankbook, Miss Graves always prepares two deposit slips, one for the bank and one to be stamped and returned to her as a receipt. When he wanted capital for a speculation, apparently Willard would withhold one check from deposit, make out new slips, and deposit the remainder of whatever Miss Graves had given him. But what he would give to her as a receipt when he returned from the bank would be the duplicate slip she had actually prepared, stamped by him instead of by the bank.'

'I see,' I said thoughtfully. 'So what you're looking for in that stack of bank statements is large amounts deposited in two separate chunks at periods up to thirty days apart, where your duplicate deposit slips show it deposited all in one piece.'

'Exactly. And so far I have discovered five instances during the past year. Amounts ranging from five thousand dollars up to the top one of seventy thousand which Willard returned yesterday.' At the thought of the seventy thousand he again ran his handkerchief over the back of his neck. 'Prior to this last time, it was mainly firm money Willard was playing with; but this belonged to a client. It was advanced to us to buy a certain stock when it falls to the price the client is willing to pay. We would have been ruined if Willard had not gotten it back in the account.'

'Happen to know what he was planning to do with the seventy thousand?' I asked.

Jones shook his head. 'Apparently he had already done it. The Riverside Bank tells me the deposit was a certified check on the Mohl and Townsend Investment Company, a competitor of ours. Willard must have bought some stock through them, then unloaded it and returned the money just before he got killed.'

'Have you talked to Mohl and Townsend?'

Again Jones shook his head. 'I don't plan to. I plan to turn all information I find in our own records over to Inspector Day and let him use it as he wishes. But beyond being thankful that his investments didn't cost Willard any money, I don't care what his speculations were now that he's dead.'

I thought about Knight's cheaply furnished frame shack, and wondered if Harlan Jones's estimate of his dead partner's luck was quite accurate. Perhaps Knight's ability to replace his borrowed money before the end of each month was no reflection of his success at speculation, and sometimes he may have had to dig deeply into his personal funds to make up the full amount.

I forbore mentioning this possibility to Jones, for his tone indicated he wanted to forget his partner's financial dealings as soon as possible. I wondered whether the disclosure of Knight's dishonesty had shaken Jones's conviction that his partner would not have made love to his wife, and whether Isobel might not be called upon to do some explaining when she awakened from her nap.

It occurred to me that the suspicion his wife had been Knight's mistress after all might be as much responsible for the state of nerves we found him in as the discovery of his narrowly averted bankruptcy.

17

The Mohl and Townsend Investment Company office was a duplicate of the Jones and Knight office with one outstanding difference. Instead of a middle-aged spinster presiding over the reception room, we found a voluptuous blonde who would have been nearly as beautiful as Fausta, had her voluptuousness not been slightly overdone.

I left her and Fausta eying each other with mutual hostility while I had a talk with the senior partner in his private office.

Alfred Mohl was a dried-up specimen of about seventy, and about as conservative as you might expect an investment broker to be. To put it mildly, he was not enthusiastic about discussing the business affairs of a client, even though the client's deceased condition made it unlikely the company would draw further business from him. Only after I had convinced him

I was working in cooperation with the homicide department, and we had reason to suspect Willard Knight's speculations somehow tied in with his murder, did he reluctantly unload.

'We have been handling transactions for Mr. Knight about three years,' he finally told me. 'Mostly of the speculative type. He was not an — ah — conservative investor.'

I asked, 'Didn't you think it strange that a rival investment broker would buy stock through you, when he easily could have done so through his own firm?'

'I sometimes wondered about it,' Mohl admitted. 'But it is not part of a broker's duty to question a client's motive for giving him business.'

'It never occurred to you Knight might be speculating with money not belonging to him?'

Alfred Mohl looked shocked. 'Certainly not!'

'Well, it seems he was. Could you tell me just what his investments were, and how he made out on each one?'

He pressed a button on his desk, and

when the large-bosomed blonde came in, asked her to bring him the file on Willard Knight. When she brought it to him, he pored over it about ten minutes while I silently smoked a cigar. Occasionally he made a note on a slip of paper.

'Here is the entire story,' he said finally, closing the file folder and handing me the paper on which he had been making notes.

Neatly divided into four columns was a list of a dozen stock transactions, the first column consisting of the names of stocks, the second the number of shares purchased, the third the purchase price, and the last the selling date and price.

A quick glance showed me the transactions were spread over a period of three years and, as Harlan Jones had guessed, each separate transaction was completed within a calendar month, making it possible for Knight to return the 'borrowed' money to the company account in time to have it included on the end-of-the-month bank statement. Ten of the transactions indicated Knight had made a profit, the smallest profit being two hundred dollars and the largest three thousand. But the other two transactions explained the cheapness of Willard Knight's home.

Between the two he had taken a loss of thirty-five thousand.

In my head I added up his wins, subtracted from his two large losses, and came out with a debit balance of approximately twenty thousand. The last transaction was the only one of the lot which showed neither profit nor loss. In the three weeks Knight had held shares, the market price had not changed a decimal.

It was the largest transaction on the list — thirty-five thousand shares of Ilco Utilities at two dollars a share. And Ilco Utilities was one of the companies in which Walter Lancaster had also been a large stockholder.

I thanked Mr. Mohl for his cooperation, collected Fausta and departed. She and the front-office blonde failed to exchange farewells, but the blonde signified her awareness of my departure with a dazzling goodbye smile. Ordinarily this would have brought a caustic remark from Fausta the moment we were outside, but apparently she was still acting the role of the skittish maiden pursued by a wolf.

Glancing at my watch, I noted that it was only a little after three. 'Day and Hannegan don't want their sleep disturbed until four,' I said. 'Let's go interrupt Isobel Jones's nap.'

Fausta raised one eyebrow. 'Isobel? I did not know you and the lady were on a first-name basis.'

'I'm an informal guy,' I growled. 'I call all my mistresses by their first names, Miss Moreni.'

We did not succeed in interrupting Isobel's nap, because she wasn't asleep when we arrived. Attired in a scanty sun suit, she was seated on the front porch sipping a highball, the color of which led me to believe it was the usual mixture of Scotch and bourbon. Fausta eyed the narrow halter and brief shorts of our hostess dubiously, unsuccessfully searched for boniness in Isobel's soft shoulders or the faint indication of wrinkles in her smooth throat, then greeted her with a sisterly smile in which there was only the barest suggestion of sororicide.

Before returning the greeting with an identically sweet smile, Isobel subjected Fausta to an equally quick but thorough examination. I never fail to be fascinated by the coldly calculating way in which beautiful women study each other whenever they encounter, and momentarily it always sends a chill along my spine. If anyone ever looked me over with the expression used by the gentler sex in examining each other, I would back into a corner with a gun in my hand.

I said, 'We thought we'd have to wake you up, Mrs. Jones. Your husband told us you meant to take a nap.'

'I planned to,' she said. 'I hardly got two hours' sleep last night, but the excitement and the ordeal of being questioned by the police has me so on edge, I doubt I'll ever sleep again. Will you people have a drink?'

Both Fausta and I shook our heads. Fausta seated herself in a canvas chair similar to the one Isobel occupied, and I sat in the green porch swing.

I said, 'I know you were answering questions all night, Mrs. Jones. But would it upset you to answer one or two more?'

'Why, no. But I told Inspector Day everything I knew about poor Willard. I couldn't sleep, you see, so I took a little walk and dropped in at the Sheridan merely because it was handy — '

'I heard that story,' I interrupted. 'Let's work on a different one. Let's go back to the night Walter Lancaster was murdered.'

She looked surprised. 'Mr. Lancaster? But obviously Willard had nothing to do with that. You don't think I did, do you?'

'No. You know you rather amaze me, Isobel. You don't seem in the least grief-stricken over Knight.'

This got me two reactions: a smoldering look from Fausta for switching to Isobel's first name, and a deprecating shrug from Isobel.

'Of course I feel terrible about it,' the latter said in a tone lacking the slightest evidence of grief. 'But after all I didn't know Willard very well. He was my husband's partner and all, but we didn't move in the same social group, and actually he was more of a friend of my husband than of me.'

I shook my head at her wonderingly. 'Isobel, you're one of the best actresses I ever encountered. In the face of all the evidence, do you really expect to convince either me or the cops you weren't carrying on an affair with Knight?'

She straightened her back indignantly. 'Why, Manny Moon! To say a thing like that in my own house! Or on the porch of my house anyway. When I tell my husband . . . '

'The cops already told him,' I said. 'He doesn't believe them, and after witnessing your convincing performance, I understand why. But I'm not your husband, and personally I don't care how many lovers you have. I also have no intention of spoiling your husband's beautiful faith in you. All I want is verification of some things I've already figured out, and only verbal verification. You don't have to sign anything, and if you object to a witness, Fausta can go inside while we talk.'

Isobel said primly, 'There is nothing I

have to say I can't say in front of a witness.'

'All right,' I said resignedly. 'Let's start with the morning after Lancaster's death. Willard Knight's wife says that when Willard saw the morning paper, at first he acted elated, then upset, and when she questioned him, he refused to tell what it was in the news that affected him, but he did remark it was a mixed blessing. Obviously what he saw was the news of Lancaster's death.'

Isobel looked politely interested, but offered no comment.

'What elated him,' I went on, 'was the realization that Lancaster had not had time before he died to make public certain irregularities he had uncovered in a firm both Knight and Lancaster held large interest in.'

Isobel said, 'I know nothing of Mr. Knight's business affairs. As a matter of fact, I don't even know anything about my husband's.'

'Then I'll bring you up to date. Knight had misappropriated seventy thousand dollars of the company's money in order to speculate, and stood to lose it if Lancaster made his announcement. Lancaster's sudden death gave him time to dispose of the stock and return the money to the company account.' I examined her for a trace of surprise, found none and asked, 'Doesn't it even worry you that Knight nearly bankrupted your husband?'

'Harlan told me about it over the phone,' she said serenely. 'Since Willard managed to return everything before he died, I can't see any cause for worry.'

I conceded that hole. 'Then we come to Knight's second reaction. When the first wave of elation passed, he became upset. And the more he thought about it, the more upset he became. Finally he grew so upset, he decided to run and hide. Know why?'

'I assume because he thought he might be suspected of the murder. I seem to recall your mentioning he had threatened Mr. Lancaster.'

'Yeah. But it wasn't only that. Innocent people don't run, even when they know they'll be suspected. Knight had two other reasons for running. First, because he couldn't afford to be delayed even for questioning until he unloaded that stock, and second because he didn't want it known where he had actually been when Lancaster was shot.'

Isobel's bored attention settled on her drink. 'He was with you, of course,' I said. 'As he probably always was when he told his wife he had a board meeting. I imagine if we got Mrs. Knight and your husband to compare notes, we'd find Willard's board meetings always coincided with your husband's trips out of town.'

She said quickly, 'I thought you weren't interested in destroying my husband's beautiful faith.'

I grinned at her. 'I'm not. I just want my hypotheses verified. When you can't get verification from one source, you try another. And beautiful as your husband's faith is, I have an idea a session with me and Mrs. Knight would shake it.' I let her absorb this a few moments, then added, 'Of course, if I could get a few halfway sensible answers out of you, it wouldn't be necessary to bring Mrs. Knight and

Harlan together.'

Isobel swished ice around in her glass, looked thoughtful, and cast a surreptitious side glance at Fausta.

'I will step into your front room,' Fausta said dryly, rising from her chair. She entered the house without glancing back at us.

Isobel continued to look thoughtful.

'Well?' I prompted.

'This won't go beyond you?' she asked.

'It won't go to your husband. It may go to the police, but I'll ask them to hold it in confidence. And if it ever gets back to your husband, you can simply say I'm a liar. I'm sure he'd believe you before he'd believe me.'

'Yes,' she agreed. 'I can handle Harlan.' She examined the swishing ice a moment longer, then said, 'It's true Willard stopped by Monday night. But it was only a social call.'

'What time did he arrive?'

'About six fifteen.'

'A quarter hour after your husband's plane left for Kansas City. How long did this social call last?'

'Well, he stayed for dinner . . . '

When her voice trailed off, I asked, 'What time did he leave?'

'Late, I guess. Rather late.'

'His wife said he got home about one a.m. That when he left?'

'Oh, no. Not that late.'

'A quarter of one?'

'I guess,' she said reluctantly. 'Along in there somewhere.'

'And you stayed here the whole time? You didn't go out?'

'Of course not. I wouldn't spend an evening out with a man who was not my husband.'

'I see,' I said. 'Was Knight gone from the house any of this time?'

She shook her head.

'You're certain? Perhaps while you were washing dishes?'

'He wiped,' Isobel said. 'He wasn't out of my sight all evening. Except . . . ' She paused.

'Except when?'

'Well, a little after nine he went down the basement for more beer because the refrigerator was empty, and was gone

238

nearly a half-hour. He got interested in Harlan's tool bench.'

'A little after nine,' I repeated. 'With perfect timing, he could have driven to El Patio, shot Lancaster and driven back again in half an hour. Could you hear him moving around in the basement?'

'No. But I know he didn't leave the house.'

'How?'

Suddenly she grinned a reckless grin straight at me. 'He didn't have any pants on. And the pants were draped over a chair within my sight all the time he was gone.'

'That settles that,' I said. 'One last question. Your meeting with Knight last night wasn't accidental at all, was it?'

'What difference does that make?'

'Just trying to make all parts of the puzzle fit. Let me guess. He phoned you to arrange the meeting, and what he wanted was to work out some story which would get him off the hook for Lancaster's murder, without disclosing he was over here with his pants off at the time Lancaster died.'

'You put it rather crudely.' Isobel frowned.

Her zany jiggling back and forth between candid admission and offended virtue began to irk me. 'You mentioned his pants first,' I said. 'Why, for cripes' sake, do you balk at admitting a planned meeting with Knight in public, after admitting he spent a pants-less six and a half hours with you in private?'

'He didn't have his pants off the whole time,' she said primly.

I scowled at her and she said, 'All right. He phoned me to meet him at the Sheridan and I sneaked out after Harlan went to sleep. We worked out a story that we had both gone to the auto races Monday night, only not together. I was going to tell the police I saw him in the crowd, but too far away to speak. The races last from eight thirty until ten thirty, so he would have been alibied for the time Mr. Lancaster was shot. After Willard died, there wasn't any point in the story, of course, because it didn't make any difference whether the police thought he killed Lancaster or not.'

I examined her face, trying to decide whether this, finally, was the truth. It was, I decided, because the reasoning was so peculiarly her own. When she said it didn't make any difference whether the police suspected a dead man of killing Lancaster or not, she meant simply that it didn't make any difference to her. The fact that settling on Knight as Lancaster's murderer would allow the real killer to go free did not concern her. Nothing concerned her which did not directly affect herself.

I climbed out of the swing. 'Thanks, Isobel. I'll keep our conversation as confidential as possible.'

'I'm sure you will,' she said, smiling up at me. 'Drop back again sometime. Without your lady friend.'

The invitation did nothing for me. It didn't flatter me, it didn't excite me, it didn't even bore me. It also hardly surprised me, for her lack of feeling over her lover's death made me realize, at least subconsciously, she would be looking for another lover before the first turned cold. I just happened to be the first man handy.

I gave her back a smile, but mine was merely polite instead of intimate. Then raising my voice, I called, 'Fausta!'

18

It was nearly four thirty when we finally got back to headquarters. Day and Hannegan were awake by then, but only barely. We found them both in the inspector's office, still rubbing sleep from their eyes.

Warren Day greeted us glumly and made a vague gesture toward a couple of chairs. Hannegan, as usual, said nothing.

When we were seated, I announced, 'I've got a brand-new theory.'

'Did you have an old one?' the inspector asked sourly.

I said, 'It's a theory I don't like very much.'

'Then don't bother me with it.'

'I don't mean it has flaws in it,' I explained. 'I don't like it for personal reasons.'

Day's expression turned faintly interested. 'Personal reasons,' he repeated. 'It can't be you feel sorry for the killer, because you don't have a heart to feel sorry with. It must be money. If your new theory is right, it's going to cost you money.'

'I wasn't thinking of that,' I said stiffly. 'I just don't like being taken for a sucker.'

'Okay. Shoot.'

'Let's start back with the meeting between Lancaster and Knight,' I said. 'According to the secretary at Jones and Knight, the two men were arguing over Lancaster's determination to make a public announcement of some irregularity he had discovered in a company they both had large investments in. It seems that company was Ilco Utilities.'

'How do you know that?'

I told him of my visits to Harlan Jones and to the Mohl and Townsend Investment Company. 'Ilco Utilities is almost certainly the company Lancaster referred to,' I went on. 'In the first place, unless Willard Knight was doing his undercover speculation through more than one investment house, Ilco Utilities was the only stock he owned. In the second place, his hurry to unload it at the same price at which he had bought indicates a panicky desire to get out from under.'

'I'll accept your premise,' the inspector said impatiently. 'You needn't belabor the point.'

'Then let's jump to Mrs. Knight's story of how her husband behaved when he saw the news of Lancaster's murder. Remember she said first he seemed elated, then frightened, and when she questioned him, he made some remark to the effect that the news was a mixed blessing.'

'She didn't say it was Lancaster's murder that set Knight off,' the inspector growled. 'She just said it was something he saw in the paper. He never told her what.'

'What else could it have been? He could hardly have missed it, since it was headlined on the front page. And his reaction was logical, since both his partner and his secretary were witnesses to the violent argument he had with Lancaster.'

'Logical unless he actually shot Lancaster.'

'He didn't,' I assured him. 'Look at it this way. The news of Lancaster's murder was entirely unexpected, and Knight's first reaction was elation that Lancaster hadn't lived long enough to make his public announcement, which gave Knight the twenty-four hours he needed to unload his stock. Then it occurred to him his argument with Lancaster made him a prime suspect and he had no alibi for the time of the murder, or at least none which would hold up under questioning. That dampened his elation, because he couldn't afford to be detained by the police even for questioning until he sold out and replaced the money he had misappropriated from the company account. Therefore he disappeared long enough to transact his business.'

'You put your own finger on the weak spot in your reasoning,' Day said. 'Knight's alibi doesn't stand up. If he had *no* alibi, I might go along. But innocent people don't fake alibis.'

I said, 'I don't claim he was innocent of everything. Only of breaking the sixth commandment. Apparently he broke the seventh repeatedly.'

The inspector looked at me blankly. Fausta, who had been sitting all this time with her hands demurely folded in her lap, interpreted for him.

'Number six is, 'Thou shalt not kill.' Number seven, 'Thou shalt not commit adultery.' Do you not read the Bible, Inspector?'

'He reads the *Police Gazette*,' I told her, then turned back to the inspector. 'Knight's fake alibi was for his wife's benefit, not an attempt to deceive the police. And I'm not spouting theory. Knight was with Isobel Jones on Monday evening from six fifteen until twelve forty-five. At her home.'

Day's eyebrows went up.

'She admitted it,' I told him. 'Of course it took me nearly ten minutes to break her down, whereas all you had was a night — '

'Get to the point, Moon!' Day roared. 'What did you get from the woman?'

So I told him.

The inspector's scowl had faded by the time I had finished, to be replaced by a thoughtful look. 'This time you think she told the truth?'

'It fits the facts too well to be another

of her fairy stories.'

Fay frowned. 'I don't quite see how this theory costs you money, Moon.'

'That wasn't a theory,' I said. 'Just some preliminary background. I'm coming to the theory now.

'The odd thing in this case so far has been an apparent lack of motive. Of course there's the remotely possible motive that Barney Seldon had Lancaster bumped as a roundabout method of avenging himself on Laurie Davis. But neither of us ever gave much credence to that, though Seldon must have some interest in the case, or he wouldn't have sicked his hood on me. Incidentally, I figure the two mugs who grabbed me this morning must have been Seldon men too, though what Barney thinks he can accomplish by having me messed up, I don't know.'

'Maybe he just doesn't like your personality,' Day growled.

Ignoring the comment, I went on, 'Then we had Knight's possible motive, but his getting killed pretty well eliminated him as a suspect even before we knew what we know now. Particularly since the attempt to poison Fausta came after Knight was dead. Only Lancaster's killer would have any reason to pass at Fausta.'

The inspector said impatiently, 'You've been talking for ten minutes since you mentioned having a brand-new theory, and you still haven't got to the point. Stop acting like a senator.'

'I'm there now, Inspector. Apparently Lancaster and Knight were the only ones who knew of the irregularities in Ilco Utilities. Both are dead. Apply the hoary old question, 'Who profits most?', and your answer is the person responsible for the irregularities. Could be the motive for both murders was simply to silence the only people who could send an embezzler to jail. Maybe if you had the Illinois police delve into Ilco Utilities, you'd find the person responsible for the irregularities and at the same time find a murderer.'

Day was silent for a long time, then: 'I think I get what you mean about this theory costing you money,' he said finally. 'Laurie Davis pay your fee in advance?'

'Just half,' I said.

'Hey!' Fausta put in. 'Laurie Davis is a friend of mine, Manny Moon. And anyway, he would not be so stupid as to hire you to catch him.'

'I've got a theory about that too,' I told her. 'Maybe all he really wanted me to do was catch up with Willard Knight. Suppose Laurie knew Lancaster was going to talk things over with Knight and then blow the top off of Ilco Utilities? And suppose he also knew Knight had disappeared after the murder and would be a logical suspect? He wants Knight located fast, and what quicker way would there be than to hire a private investigator? He doesn't have to say, 'Find Willard Knight for me,' because as the most logical suspect, he knows the investigator will go after Knight first. So he hires me ostensibly to find a killer, puts Farmer Cole on my tail, and when I locate Knight, the Farmer rubs him out.'

'Wait a minute,' the inspector said. 'We didn't know Knight had disappeared even here at headquarters until you gave us the tip.'

'But Laurie may have. He had been checking into the case before he came to see me, because he knew all about Barney Seldon being questioned and released. Why don't you check Mrs. Knight, and Harlan Jones, and his secretary, Matilda Graves, to see if anyone made some inquiries before I did? And Laurie *did* put Farmer Cole on my tail. To protect me, according to the Farmer, which is a bit of thoughtfulness that seems out of character for Mr. Davis.'

Fausta said, 'No one was trailing us last night when Mr. Knight was killed.'

I emitted an unamused laugh. 'Farmer Cole knows how to stay invisible. He was on me a whole day, and the only two times I spotted him were the two times he wanted me to.'

Day said, 'I think I'm going to buy your new theory, Moon. But Davis isn't the kind of guy you can pull in on suspicion. Before we go any further, I'm going to ask the Illinois police to look over Ilco Utilities.' He reached for his phone.

I said, 'I just had an idea that might tell us quicker if we're on the right track. Let me make a call first.'

The inspector took his hand away from the phone, leaned back in his chair and watched me while I looked up the number of the Mohl and Townsend Investment Company in the phone book. I gave it to the switchboard operator and a moment later was talking to old Mr. Mohl.

After explaining I was in the office of the chief of Homicide, I asked if he had any information as to who were the directors of Ilco Utilities. He left me holding the phone nearly five minutes before he came back and began reeling off a list of a dozen names. One of the names was Laurence Davis.

I thanked him and was about to hang up when he cleared his throat and said in his dried-up voice, 'A person was in making inquiries about you shortly after you left here, Mr. Moon.'

'A person?'

'I didn't see him myself. He talked only to our receptionist. He claimed he was a friend of yours, had seen you enter the building and was trying to find you. But the manner in which he asked questions convinced the lady he was trying to pump her about what your business had been.'

'She tell him?'

'No. She suggested he talk to me, but he said that wouldn't be necessary and departed.'

'Leave a name?' I asked.

'No. But she describes him as tall and rather thin.'

'She mention his teeth?'

'His teeth?' Alfred Mohl paused in thought, then said, 'She did, now that you remind me. Rather protruding, she said.'

I said, 'Thanks a lot, Mr. Mohl. I know the man.'

I hung up and told Warren Day, 'Farmer Cole is still on me. He walked into Mohl and Townsend right after we left and tried to find out what I wanted there.'

'That disproves your whole theory,' Fausta said. 'If he was following you simply because he wanted to kill Mr. Knight, he would have stopped after accomplishing his mission. Probably Laurie Davis has him following you to make sure you do not loaf.'

Ignoring her, I asked Day, 'What do you make of that?'

The inspector shook his head. 'Nothing. It doesn't make sense. Was Davis on the list of directors?'

'Yeah. So maybe you better make that call to the Illinois police.'

It was shortly after five when we left headquarters, and Fausta demanded a cocktail.

'You have dragged me here, there and everywhere all afternoon,' she said. 'But you have hardly even looked at me. Now it is time to forget work and concentrate on me.'

I took her to the Jefferson because it was close to headquarters, found an empty booth and ordered a rum-and-Coke and a rye with water. When the waiter brought them, he also brought a third glass that looked as if it contained Tom Collins.

I said, 'We ordered only two drinks.'

'The gentleman at the cigarette machine,' he said, nodding toward a man who was in the act of dropping a quarter in the slot. 'He said he was joining you and paid for all three drinks.'

The man was Farmer Cole.

He sauntered over, tearing the red tab from his cigarette package, nodded to Fausta, looked at me without expression, and slid into the booth on Fausta's side.

I asked, 'Know the gentleman, Fausta?'

'Oh, yes,' Fausta said. 'Mr. Cole frequently dines at El Patio with Laurie Davis.'

I raised my glass. 'Thanks for the drink, Farmer.'

'A pleasure.' Suddenly he pulled his cigarette trick again, popping one into his mouth and getting a lighted match under it in a blur of motion too fast to follow.

I said, 'One day you're going to scorch the end of your nose doing that.'

'It's my nose,' he said in a reasonable tone.

'Yeah,' I agreed. 'But it seems to spend a lot of time in my business. Got a plausible explanation for keeping on my tail constantly?'

'Not constantly,' he demurred. 'Only periodically. And I told you why. Boss's orders.'

'Why the orders?'

His bony shoulders moved in a shrug. 'I'm just common labor. I don't ask why. You'd have to go to management to find out.'

'I'll do that,' I told him. 'I think I need a talk with Mr. Davis.'

'Yes, you do. That's why I intruded on your little tête-à-tête. Tuesday Mr. Davis left you his phone number, with instructions to call in any progress. This is Thursday, and he's beginning to wonder why the phone doesn't ring.'

'There hasn't been any progress. Except negative.'

'You mean you've eliminated some possibilities? Even that would interest Mr. Davis.' He examined me with his mouth open for a moment. 'Suppose you give me a brief run-down; I'll pass it on, and you won't have to bother phoning Mr. Davis.'

'Sure,' I said. 'Willard Knight didn't shoot Lancaster. Neither did Warren Day, Fausta or I. End of report.'

'Very concise, Mr. Moon. What did you find out at Mohl and Townsend?'

'The receptionist is single, but she leans backward when she runs. Alfred

Mohl believes in gilt-edged securities and votes Republican.'

The look he gave me was the same one he had employed the first time we met. Not belligerent, nor threatening, but merely a quietly informative look which let me know if I wanted a contest, he would gladly tear off one of my arms and beat me over the head with it.

I said, 'I don't deal with common labor. I'll get in touch with top management.'

'Yes, do that,' he said quietly.

Lifting his glass for the first time, he drained it in one continuous swallow, rose from his seat, inclined his head at Fausta and sauntered off.

19

That evening Don Bell, the local radio gossip, had the full story of Fausta's narrow escape from poisoning on his nine o'clock broadcast. I was rather surprised, inasmuch as the evening papers had carried nothing but the bare announcement of the waiter's death, with the additional information that the police were investigating.

Apparently Warren Day, for reasons of his own, had not wanted the incident publicly connected with the Lancaster and Knight murders, but there had been the usual leak resulting in a Don Bell exclusive. If the inspector was listening to the broadcast, he'd be pretty riled, I reflected.

Fausta's phone rang just as the broadcast ended, and Fausta went into her bedroom to answer it. When she returned to the front room, she announced, 'That was Lieutenant Hannegan. Inspector Day wants you to meet him at your apartment right away. The inspector is already on his way, and Lieutenant Hannegan has been phoning everywhere trying to reach you.'

'Hannegan said all that?' I asked, surprised. 'Usually he isn't so voluble.'

Then, not because I had the least suspicion the call was faked, but merely from the habit of double-checking, I went into the bedroom and phoned headquarters. Since both Day and Hannegan went off duty at five, I was not surprised to find neither there. The sergeant on duty at Homicide knew nothing about their whereabouts.

I tried Day's apartment, but when the phone had rung six times without answer, hung up. Then I tried my own number, and again hung up after six rings. Apparently Day had not yet arrived, for while I kept my apartment locked, the apartment manager knew the inspector well enough to let him in with a passkey, and I was certain Day would not stand out in the hall waiting when he could just as easily be inside drinking up my rye.

I made one more call, to the bar phone downstairs, and this time I got an answer.

I told the bartender to send up Mouldy Greene.

When I returned to the front room, Fausta was freshening her lipstick with the obvious intention of going out.

I said, 'You're staying right here in this nice safe apartment.'

'I thought you were going to protect me twenty-four hours a day,' Fausta said. 'Suppose that was not Lieutenant Hannegan at all, but the killer trying to lure you away so I would be alone?'

'You won't be alone. Mouldy's coming up. And wasn't it Hannegan?'

Fausta shrugged. 'I suppose. I haven't heard him speak more than twice, and never over the phone.'

'I'm reasonably sure it was the lieutenant,' I assured her. 'Warren Day is out, and he rarely goes anywhere except on business. He hates spending the money on foolish things like women and strong drink. His idea of a good time is to run down to the bank and deposit his paycheck. And since the banks aren't open at this time of night, he must be out on business. Anyway, if our killer was

260

trying to get at you, he'd probably assume I was dragging you along, and plan to pot you from some ambush.'

'Why not have the inspector come here?'

I said, 'In the first place I can't reach him. In the second, he'd only swear at me and tell me to get home fast even if I did reach him. And in the third place, I forgot my pajamas and toothbrush, so I can kill two birds with one stone.'

'It is too hot to sleep in pajamas,' Fausta said. 'And you may share my toothbrush.'

'Stop acting like a suspicious wife,' I told her. 'You'd think we were on a honeymoon and I was trying to sneak out with the boys.'

Mouldy arrived at that moment. I told him he was Fausta's bodyguard until I got back and I wanted him in the apartment with the door locked.

'How about my job?' he asked. 'Nobody's on the door.'

'The customers will just have to put up with a bow from the head waiter instead of a slap on the back from you,' I said.

'You stay here and don't unlock that door for anyone but me.'

As Mouldy's single military efficiency had been guard duty, I felt no qualms about leaving Fausta in his custody. As a sentinel he followed orders implicitly, his sole drawback being lack of flexibility. Having been instructed not to unlock the door, he wouldn't unlock it even if the place caught fire, nor would he permit Fausta to. So while there was a remote possibility I would return to find both Mouldy and Fausta roasted alive, I could be reasonably certain no killers would get to Fausta while I was gone.

I left my car in the 'no parking' space in front of my apartment inasmuch as I was on police business, and I have noticed the police pay little attention to parking regulations when on official business. As I expected, I found my front door unlocked, but when I opened it, the front room was dark.

Assuming the inspector was in the kitchen investigating my refrigerator, I pushed the door shut behind me and felt for the wall switch in the dark. When light sprang into the room, I found myself looking into the familiar bore of a short-barreled revolver.

The flat-faced pseudocop who had dumped me in the center of Midland Park sat in my favorite easy chair, and it was he who held the gun. His driver, Slim, reclined on the couch with his feet on my cocktail table.

Before I got over my surprise, I heard myself saying, 'Get your oversized shoes off that table!'

Startled, Slim dropped his feet to the floor, then scowled at me and rose from the sofa.

'You should be more careful of other people's property,' his flat-faced friend admonished him. Apologetically he explained to me, 'Slim never had much bringing up. And sitting here in the dark, I never noticed what he was doing.' His pistol bored unwaveringly at the center of my stomach.

I asked, 'Which one of you is Lieutenant Hannegan?'

'Slim,' Flat-face said. 'Slim can be real clever when he manages to stay awake.'

Slim growled something and his partner went on, 'You wouldn't believe it, but the whole idea was Slim's. Phoning Warren Day to make sure he wasn't home, in case you got suspicious and checked back. Imitating Lieutenant Hannegan to Miss Moreni. Ain't he a little genius?'

'Shut up and let's get going,' Slim said.

'Sure,' Flat-face said. His tone shed its mock politeness. 'Turn around with your hands on top of your head, buster.'

Since the order was accompanied by the snick of his revolver hammer being drawn back, I turned around and clasped my hands atop my head. An instant later his left hand snaked under my armpit from behind and removed my P-38. I heard it clank as it was laid on the mantel.

'Let's go,' Flat-face said, prodding my spine with the cocked revolver.

Assuming he meant go outside, I opened the door and preceded both of them. I continued to lead down the half-flight to the main entrance, out to the street, which, as was usual for that time of night in my neighborhood, was deserted, and across the street to the blue sedan parked there.

Following instructions, I got in the back, where I was joined by the man with the gun. Slim took the wheel.

I said, 'It may be a shock to you, but I haven't the vaguest idea who you guys are, or what you think you're accomplishing by kidnaping me every few hours.'

'Not kidnaping, buster,' my seatmate said quickly. 'Abducting.'

Although the distinction seemed unnecessary hair-splitting, and his correction a bit too quick, I let it pass. 'Do you fellows just get a kick out of dumping people off places so they have to walk home?'

'This time we ain't dumping you.'

'Your plans a secret?'

'Just shut up, buster. You'll find out soon enough.'

Since he said this in a tone indicating the alternative to my shutting up might be a bump on the head, and accompanied the words with a hefting of his revolver, as though preparing to use it as a club, I shut up. At a moderate speed Slim drove along side streets in the direction of the river. At that time of night bridge traffic was slight, and we made the approach to the bridge without even having to shift gears.

In the center of the bridge, I chanced further conversation. 'Kidnaping and crossing a state line,' I commented. 'You boys are so brave, thumbing your noses at the FBI like this.'

'You don't know your laws,' Flat-face growled. 'Kidnaping is when you steal somebody and keep him. It's only abduction if you just steal him temporary-like. And who the hell would want to keep a blabbermouth like you?'

So it was not a death ride, I thought. I found the thought cheering, but it did nothing to sate my curiosity.

I said, 'Whoever hired you for this sold you a bill of goods. Abduction, as a legal term, applies only to women. You've just committed two federal offenses: kidnaping and crossing a state line during the commission of a felony. But you'll have lots of time to explain you thought it was only abduction. About forty years.'

In the front seat Slim said thoughtfully,

'If this guy is right, maybe we better bump him, huh?'

I said hastily, 'Of course if I didn't make a complaint, you wouldn't be in any trouble. And if we turned around and went home, naturally I wouldn't have anything to complain about.'

'Why don't you shut up?' Flat-face inquired in a bored tone.

So I shut up for the rest of the ride. It wasn't long, for our destination was Maddon, and a four-lane highway leads almost from the bridge ramp on the Illinois side straight to the place. Within ten minutes of the time we left the bridge we were pulling into the driveway of a neat white cottage on the outskirts of the little town.

At a prod from the revolver, I climbed out of the car and preceded my companions to a side door. Stepping ahead of me, Slim opened the door and led the way into a small hallway. When he gestured me on, I followed past an open doorway through which I caught a glimpse of a tastefully furnished living room; then we turned left into a narrower hallway and marched toward

267

the rear of the house. Just short of the kitchen Slim opened another door and led me down a flight of stairs to the basement. During the whole journey Flat-face stayed one step behind me with the barrel of his pistol almost touching my back.

The basement, or at least that part of it we found ourselves in, had been converted into a large playroom. The ceiling was white acoustic board, the walls unstained knotty pine, and the floor alternate black and red squares of asphalt tile. In one corner was a bleached-oak bar before which stood a half-dozen red leather stools, and behind which was a back bar containing at least fifty bottles. Diagonally across from it in the corner was a round poker table with a green felt top. The other two corners respectively contained a regulation-size pool table and a jukebox. Two slot machines against the wall, a TV console, a couple of small round cocktail tables and a number of chrome-and-leather chairs completed the furnishings.

Other than we three new arrivals, only one person occupied the playroom. Attired in formal pants, a purple smoking jacket and leather loafers, Barney Seldon sat on one of the bar stools watching television. The moment we entered, he jerked a thumb at the television screen. Slim walked over and cut off one of TV's highest-paid comics in the middle of a gag.

Seldon said, 'Evening, Mr. Moon,' drained the highball before him, and lit a cigarette with a gold lighter. Frowning at his two hirelings, he said, 'Took you long enough.'

'After we phoned you about that business this morning we never had a chance,' Flat-face explained. 'He was stuck to Miss Moreni all day, and we figured you wouldn't want us pulling nothing with her around. We finally pried him out of her apartment with a fake call.'

Barney Seldon's face darkened as he swung toward me. I felt mine darken too, but more with shame than with anger. That Farmer Cole had been tailing me without my being able to spot him I knew, but the Farmer had been trained by the FBI. The discovery that two run-of-the-mill hoods had also managed to stay on me all day without detection touched my vanity where it hurt.

I took a bar stool a seat or two away from Seldon, leaned my back against the bar and made a point of slowly studying the room. Slim seated himself at the poker table and idly shuffled a deck of cards. Flat-face leaned against the pool table, his gun still in his hand and still cocked.

Barney examined me coldly and finally said, 'You were a little bit rough on my boy, Percy Sweet.'

'Tit for tat,' I told him. 'Percy tried to be a little rough on me.'

'And then you yelled cop,' Barney said. 'Really, I was a little disappointed. Fausta built you up as such a tough guy, but instead of fighting your own battles, you yell cop.'

I looked at him in astonishment. 'My own battles? When you try to scare me off a murder case, it isn't a simple matter of Moon versus Seldon. It becomes Seldon versus the People.'

Barney's eyebrows went up. 'Murder case? You talking about the Lancaster affair?'

'That and Willard Knight. You had

anyone else bumped recently?'

Barney laughed a short unpleasant laugh. 'Is that why you think you're on my stink list?'

I merely looked at him without answering.

'What did Percy say to you?' he asked.

I simulated his short, unpleasant laugh. 'He intimated in his terse, ungrammatical way that he was going to learn me to kick a field goal, my head being the ball. And the lesson was to teach me to stay out of your hair.'

'No explanation of how you got in my hair?'

I shook my head. 'Since our sole contact concerned Walter Lancaster, I assumed my looking into his murder ruffled your toupee.'

Barney snorted smoke in my direction. 'We also discussed a lady.'

For a moment I didn't get it, and when I finally did, it filled me with such a mixture of disgust and rage, I slid from my stool and reached out to gather a fistful of smoking jacket.

Across the room Flat-face said tonelessly, 'You'll get a slug in your guts.'

That deterred me from slugging Barney, but did nothing to abate my anger. Gripping the seat of the bar stool between us instead of his jacket, I leaned toward him and said impolitely, 'You underdeveloped cretin! I'm up to my neck in a double murder investigation, trying to prevent a third, and you bother me with a lot of teenage nonsense over a girl! In grammar school, boys sic their gangs on fellows who mess with their girls, but they outgrow such juvenile stuff by the time they get to high school. Of course, never having attended either one, a paleolithic moron like you wouldn't know that, but — '

'Hold it, Moon!' Barney said in a strangled voice.

'You ape-brained simpleton!' I yelled. 'Grown men don't win women by having their rivals beat up. What in hell do you think you're accomplishing with this nonsense?'

Leaving his stool, Barney gripped the opposite side of the same one I was gripping and put his handsome nose an inch from mine. 'I'm going to marry that girl! That's what I'm accomplishing!' he yelled back at me. 'And I'm keeping you away from her if I have to beat your brains out every hour on the hour!'

I straightened up. 'She wouldn't have a triple-plated jerk like you if you had every man in a radius of fifty miles beaten up.'

That released his trigger. Stepping away from the bar, he started a fast left hook at my head. Unfortunately for him, this put him between me and the gun in Flat-face's hand. Deflecting his hook with my open right palm, I leaned my back against the bar, brought up my aluminum foot, planted it in his groin and snapped my leg straight. He shot across the room on his heels, crashed into Flat-face and took him to the floor with him.

I was vaulting the bar while Slim dropped his cards, leaped to his feet and began to reach under his coat. With a pinch bottle of Scotch in one hand and a quart of Irish whisky in the other, I spun toward him and hurled the former end-over-end just as his gun began to clear. The Irish I flipped two feet lower an instant later.

Slim ducked the Scotch just in time to catch the Irish squarely on the nose. The pinch bottle burst all over the wall behind him, but the Irish didn't even break. It rolled one way, Slim rolled the other, then both lay still.

The instant the Irish left my hand, I was re-armed again, this time with a square bottle of gin and a quart of bourbon. Both started toward the corner containing the pool table just as Barney rolled from Flat-face's lap. Seated spread-eagled on the floor, Flat-face tried to duck and fire at the same time. Both bottles missed, but so did his bullet, burying itself somewhere in the ceiling above me.

Before Flat-face could align his sights for a second shot, I had two more bottles started, and after that I kept them going as rapidly as a juggler throws Indian clubs. It is amazing how accurately you can toss a full quart bottle clear across a room. In spite of hardly taking time to aim, not one of the eighteen quarts I threw missed Barney or Flat-face more than two feet. After the second volley

Flat-face gave up trying to get in a shot, and he and Barney devoted themselves to scampering about on all fours in a frantic attempt to dodge the rain of hard drinks.

Had they kept out of each other's way, perhaps all the bottles would have missed, but they were both paying more attention to me than to where they were going, and they met head on just in time for the seventeenth bottle to catch them right where their heads were touching. The eighteenth I had already started by then, and it sailed harmlessly over their prone figures to burst against the windows of one of the one-armed bandits. Had this final bottle connected with either of the men, I would have had a corpse on my hands, for it seemed to possess more steam than my earlier throws. It was hard enough to disrupt the mechanism of the slot machine, for the machine emitted a dull clanking noise, slowly turned its left-hand drum until a lemon showed, and spit dimes all over the floor.

The floor was a mess. Counting the two bottles I had thrown at Slim, I had fired twenty quarts and all but four had broken. Four gallons of mixed liquor trickled over broken glass and filled the air with an overpoweringly rich aroma.

Rolling both Flat-face and Barney on their backs to prevent them from drowning in a puddle of whisky, I examined them and decided neither probably suffered anything more dangerous than mild concussion. Slim was going to require some plastic work on his nose and possibly had a fractured skull, but he also was alive.

For a few moments I contemplated the recumbent figure of Barney Seldon, wondering what I had better do about him. I realized he would regard this incident only as further reason for having his goons teach me a lesson, and the prospect of permanently keeping one eye over my shoulder did not appeal to me. After some thought I picked Flat-face's pistol off the floor, wiped it clean of liquor and thrust it in my coat pocket. Relieving Slim of the keys to the blue sedan, I pocketed them also. Then I found an ice bucket behind the bar, filled it with water and dumped it in Barney's face.

After the second bucket, he woke up. Spluttering, the gang leader sat erect, groaned and pressed both hands to the side of his head where the seventeenth bottle had caught him. A noticeable bump was beginning to form. When I judged the bells in his head had reduced their jangle sufficiently for him to understand words, I said, 'Barney!' He looked up slowly, still holding his head, and blinked at me. 'Barney, can you understand me?'

He started to nod his head, but the movement brought a moan from his lips. Thickly he said, 'Yes.'

'Then listen carefully. I don't care how hard you chase Fausta, because when she gets tired of your chasing, she's perfectly capable of tying a can to your tail without my help. And if I feel like it, I'll chase her too. Without your permission. But keep your goons away from me.'

He said something under his breath.

'Understand this clearly, Barney. I've no intention of spending the rest of my life jumping at shadows. One more pass at me and I'm coming at you with a gun. Not after your hoods, but straight at you.

And if you think that won't get you dead, check the morgue records over my way.'

Still clasping both hands to his head, Barney said indistinctly, 'I know you've knocked off a bad boy or two, Moon.'

'Mr. Moon.'

After a pause he sulkily amended, 'Mr. Moon.'

'Want to call it quits, Barney, or want to make this a real feud?'

His glazed eyes peered up at me with hate, but after an imperceptible hesitation, he said, 'I guess a dame's not important enough to kill a guy over, and I'd have to kill you if you came gunning.'

'Think you could?' I asked.

'I don't want to,' he said with a mixture of pain and irritation. 'All I ever intended was to give you a few bumps, but you got to take things serious. Just go away and leave me alone.'

I left him alone amid the ruins of his playroom and his two hoods.

20

I left Flat-face's pistol in the glove compartment of the blue sedan, and the sedan I abandoned with the keys in it across the street from my apartment in the same spot my visitors had previously parked it. On my own car I found a parking ticket, of course, over an hour and a half having elapsed since I left it in the 'no parking' zone. I filed the ticket in my breast pocket for later presentation to Warren Day.

My front door had been left unlocked, but apparently I had received no other visitors, for things were exactly as they had been left. I recovered my P-38 from the mantel, rolled my pajamas into a tight package with my toothbrush inside, and was out of the flat again within two minutes.

Fausta, attired in a thin but opaque white dressing gown which hid all but the bottom six inches of a startlingly transparent nightgown, was amusing Mouldy by letting him watch her paint her toenails when I finally got back. This I gathered not from observation, but from deduction, for by the time I had convinced Mouldy through the locked door that it was really I and I was alone, Fausta had completed the job. When Mouldy finally let me in, she had her tiny feet on a footstool and was wriggling them in an apparent attempt to make them dry faster.

The moment I entered, Fausta wrinkled her nose and said, 'Are you drunk, Manny?'

I said, 'You're acting more and more like a wife. Keep it up and I'll start insisting on the pleasures of marriage as well as the inconveniences.'

'You will?' she asked in an interested voice. Then she screwed up her nose again. 'You smell like a distillery. Have you been swimming in the stuff?'

'Just wading,' I told her, for the first time becoming conscious of the aroma I was carrying about with me.

Examining my shoes, I discovered they were soaked above the insole with liquor. Kicking them off, I carried them over to the open window and set them on the sill to dry.

'You can get back to your back-slapping,' I told Mouldy.

'Sure, Sarge. Where'd you find liquor deep enough to wade in?'

'Barney Seldon's, over in Maddon.'

Fausta said, 'Barney Seldon? You were over at his place tonight, Manny?'

'Yeah. And your handsome boyfriend is out as a murder suspect. The two hoods who dumped me in Midland Park were Barney's boys, incidentally, and their original intention was the same as Percy Sweet's. To beat me up. But it turns out Barney was just jealous about me chasing you, and knows nothing of the Lancaster killing. Apparently the reason the hoods changed their minds about beating me up was that they knew Barney would regard your welfare as more important, and they dumped me out in order to run to your rescue. I assume that when they found cops already on the scene, they quietly faded out of sight.'

Fausta said indignantly, 'Wait until that Barney Seldon comes here again!'

'I don't think he'll try any more passes at me,' I said. 'We talked the matter over and he agreed he was being childish.'

Fausta looked at me suspiciously. 'You beat him up,' she accused.

'I didn't lay a hand on him,' I said truthfully.

Mouldy asked, 'How come you were wading in liquor?'

'Barney has a stream of it running right through his house.'

Mouldy looked surprised. 'That jerk? A real whisky stream?'

'A real whisky stream.'

'What do you know?' Mouldy said. 'A jerk like Romeo Seldon striking whisky. Luck never happens to guys who deserve it.'

'Try drilling under your bed,' I suggested. 'Maybe you'll strike a Martini spring.'

'Now you're kidding,' Mouldy said. 'Everybody knows Martinis aren't raw products like whisky. You mix gin and vamoose.'

'Yeah, do that. Vamoose, I mean. I'll take over Fausta's protection.'

When the door closed behind Mouldy, Fausta asked, 'Who is supposed to protect me against you?'

'Your virtue, my honor and the lock on your bedroom door. Not to mention my state of near-collapse after a hard day.'

Fausta watched broodingly as I stripped back the daybed and plumped my pillow into shape. Giving her toes a final wriggle, she stretched like a kitten and came erect. 'Good night, Manny,' she said politely.

I said, 'Good night, Fausta,' in an equally polite voice, but as she padded by on bare feet, I suddenly grabbed her by the shoulders and swung her against my chest.

Far from being surprised, she met me as though expecting the maneuver. Using my ears as handles, she pulled my mouth down to hers and kept it there until smoke began to curl from between us. Then with a side twist as efficient as a shifty halfback's, she slipped from my arms and scooted into her bedroom. The door closed, but I heard no sound of a key turning.

Slowly I undressed, donned my pajamas and took my time getting two drinks mixed. I was starting toward the door with the drinks in my hands when it suddenly opened.

There was no light behind Fausta, but the front room was brightly lighted. The vision stopped me in my tracks, and I was still standing there foolishly with my hands full of highball glasses when she grinned like a gamin, gently closed the door in my face and locked it.

Setting both glasses on an end table, I tried the knob without success.

Bitterly I said through the door, 'A woman who does things like that deserves to be hanged by the thumbs.'

There was a pause, then, 'Want to marry me?'

'Oh, the hell with it,' I said, and retreating to the end table, drank both drinks one after the other.

As Fausta had warned, the daybed was not very comfortable.

The smell of frying bacon aroused me at the ungodly hour of eight a.m. Strapping on my leg, I shrugged on a robe, visited the bathroom long enough to brush my teeth, then went to investigate the smell.

I found Fausta before the stove fully dressed, if you could call the fraction of a yard of blue cotton comprising her sunsuit fully dressed. Greeting me cheerily, just as though nothing out of the way had occurred between us the previous night, she set a steaming cup of coffee before me.

'Eggs and bacon in five minutes,' she said, and returned to the stove

After breakfast, with Fausta in tow, I arrived at Warren Day's office about nine a.m. The inspector looked up in simulated astonishment when we walked in.

'Still up from last night?' he asked. 'You wouldn't get up this early without a summons, so you must not have been to bed.'

I told him I had been asleep by midnight, and tossed my parking ticket on his desk.

Before he had a chance to refuse it, I said, 'I got it on police business, and the business paid off. You may scratch Barney Seldon off your list of suspects.'

The abrupt way in which I made this announcement made Day blink. 'What?'

'Barney Seldon.' I gave him a brief run-down of my previous evening's activities. 'So you may as well tear up that assault complaint against Percy Sweet and Seldon at the same time you tear up my ticket,' I concluded. 'You only wanted it as an excuse to hold Seldon when you got your hands on him anyway. And since both Barney and Percy Sweet are clear on the Lancaster and Knight killings, I'm not interested in pressing charges.'

The inspector scratched his long nose. 'Suppose Barney was selling you a bill of goods?'

'He wasn't,' I assured him. 'Aside from the fact that our killer tried to poison Fausta, which Barney would certainly never do, his hoods dumping me and scurrying to Fausta's rescue the minute they learned she was in danger cinches it that Seldon was merely behaving like a jealous juvenile delinquent. And don't tell me his actions were too childish to be plausible. You have to possess subnormal intelligence to be a hood in the first place.'

Reluctantly the inspector agreed with

me. Apparently his reluctance stemmed from this leaving him only Laurie Davis as a suspect, whereas he would have preferred someone with less influence. Not that political influence could deter Warren Day an inch from what he regarded as his duty, even though it did tend to awe him, but from a practical point of view it made his task harder.

Seldon he could have dragged in, placed under a white light and hammered with questions until he was groggy. With Laurie Davis he would have to have an airtight case before even approaching the man.

Hannegan stuck his head in the door, cocked an eyebrow at Day, and the inspector shook his head at him.

'Cancel it,' Day said. 'I decided to go myself.'

Hannegan looked a mute inquiry.

'Why the hell can't you talk?' Day blared at him. 'I'm tired of your sign language.'

'Yes, sir,' Hannegan said. His head disappeared and the door closed.

Rising from behind his desk, Day

reached for his flat straw hat.

'Where you bound?' I asked.

'Over to the Jones and Knight Company,' he said without enthusiasm. 'Come along if you want.'

The very fact that he issued an invitation convinced me he considered the visit unimportant. I asked, 'What's up?'

The inspector grimaced. 'Jones phoned. He's completed the examination of his books. He has all the data concerning Knight's borrowings listed.'

His indifferent tone told me he had decided everything connecting Knight's death to Lancaster's had been uncovered when we ran into Ilco Utilities, but he could not pass up the remote chance of finding something which might point toward a less troublesome suspect than the political boss of Illinois. His treatment of Lieutenant Hannegan verified this reasoning also. Apparently he had instructed the lieutenant to make the trip to Jones and Knight Company, but changed his mind when he lost Barney Seldon as a suspect. The chief of Homicide personally going on such a routine errand indicated the inspector had reached the point of desperately grasping at straws. Having reached the same point myself, I told him we would go along.

This time when we arrived at the Jones and Knight Investment Company, Matilda Graves was not crying. She was filing letters, and she was being very brisk and businesslike for the benefit of the remaining partner's wife. Isobel Jones sat in one of the three visitors' chairs, watching her with amused disinterest.

The secretary-bookkeeper greeted Fausta and me, then looked inquiringly at Warren Day.

'Day of Homicide,' the inspector growled at her.

'Oh, yes, officer. Mr. Jones was expecting someone from the police, but he is in conference at the moment. I'm sure he'll be through in a matter of minutes now. Do you mind waiting?'

It was obvious from the inspector's expression that he not only minded, but considered the suggestion preposterous. As chief of Homicide he was used to others waiting on his convenience, and reversal of the usual procedure caught him off center. But it was equally obvious Matilda Graves had no idea she was speaking to the chief of Homicide, and assumed he was merely a plainclothes policeman. Since he could hardly correct her impression without sounding pompous, he grunted something unintelligible, seated himself in the visitor's chair farthest from Isobel Jones, and glanced at her obliquely. As usual he covered his unease at the presence of an attractive woman with a fierce scowl.

Isobel said, 'Hello, Manny,' nodded at Fausta, and favored the inspector with a dazzling smile.

With his eyes on Matilda Graves, who was too plain to upset him, Day muttered, 'Morning, Mrs. Jones.'

I said, 'Can't even the wives of businessmen get in to see them when they're in conference?'

'Not when they're in conference with lawyers, apparently. This seems to have been a bad day to call for shopping money.'

Fausta had seated herself between

Isobel and Day, which left me standing, as there were no more chairs.

'Why don't you bring a chair from Mr. Knight's office,' Isobel suggested. 'I've had experience with Harlan's 'few minutes' before, and sometimes they stretch.'

After another ten minutes of standing, I crossed to the door of Knight's office. Apparently the partition between the two rooms was thin, for the moment I opened the door I could hear the murmur of conversation through the wall. Although muffled, I could make out the words without difficulty.

A husky voice I at first thought was that of a man, but almost immediately identified as that of Mrs. Knight, was saying, 'I don't see that Willard's borrowing has any bearing on the subject, since he returned every cent. It was an equal partnership, wasn't it? So why should I accept less than half the firm's value as estimated by an independent appraiser?'

A suave voice I assumed belonged to the lawyer mentioned by Isobel began an explanation. 'The total estimated worth of a business of this nature has to be based

291

on two factors, Mrs. Knight. There is first the intrinsic value of office fixtures and equipment, monies and securities belonging to the firm. Things upon which an accurate monetary value may be fixed. But the other factor is intangible. It consists of customer lists, the firm's reputation in financial circles, the sales ability of firm members and so on. In this case a large part of this intangible value rests on the last item, the sales ability of the members. Now your husband was an excellent salesman, but obviously this ceased to be an asset to the firm the moment he passed away.'

'How about the customer list?' Mrs. Knight asked sullenly. 'Didn't Willard build that up as much as you did?'

Apparently this was addressed to Harlan Jones, for after clearing his throat, Jones's voice said, 'Yes, of course. It's only fair to concede that.'

'But on the other hand,' the lawyer smoothly interjected, 'your husband's — ah — borrowing firm funds undoubtedly will have some adverse effect on the firm's business. Rumors certainly will spread, particularly since a rival investment house knows of the — ah — borrowing. And while to some extent these rumors may be offset by the general knowledge that the borrower is no longer active in the firm, you must concede this would not be the case were Mr. Knight still alive. Therefore I think it hardly would be fair to consider the firm's reputation among the intangibles in arriving at an estimated value.'

Obviously the man was Harlan Jones's lawyer instead of Mrs. Knight's, I thought. And he was good. At least the short snatch of conversation I overheard had me convinced Jones should be allowed to buy out his partner's interest for less than half the appraised value of the business.

That is, it had me convinced while I was listening. After returning to the reception room with a straight-backed chair I found in Knight's office, and thinking over what I had heard, I retained only my first opinion: that the lawyer was good. When you delved beneath his plausible arguments, the fact remained that Knight and

Jones had owned equal interest in the business. And if Jones wanted to buy out Knight's heir, the fairest price was half the value of the business.

Then another thought occurred to me. Why was the division of the business being rushed, and who was doing the rushing, Jones or Mrs. Knight? Willard Knight had been dead less than forty-eight hours. As a matter of fact, due to the delay attendant on an autopsy, I imagined he had not yet even had a funeral. Who was so eager to divide up the business that the matter could not wait until Knight was buried?

21

I said to Isobel, 'You didn't mention Mrs. Knight was in there with your husband.'

She raised her eyebrows. 'Should I have?' Then she asked curiously, 'How did you know she was?'

'Thin walls,' I said.

Warren Day said restlessly, 'How long are we going to have to wait, miss?'

The question was addressed to Matilda, who said, 'I'm sure it won't be long, officer. I buzzed Mr. Jones that you were here.'

At that moment Harlan Jones opened his office door to glance out, his eyes widened when he spotted the inspector and he hurried over to him. 'I had no idea it was you waiting, sir,' he said, nervously shaking Day's hand. 'Miss Graves merely announced a policeman.'

Jones smiled skittishly at Fausta, nodded to me and gave a preoccupied greeting to his wife. 'I'm afraid I'll be tied up for some time, Inspector,' he went on.

'Suppose we step into my ex-partner's office to go over what I've been able to unearth. My other visitors can wait in mine.'

Isobel said, 'While you're here, dear . . . '

'Oh, yes,' Jones said. Self-consciously, while we all looked on, he extracted what looked like two fifties from his wallet and handed the bills to his wife.

Jones moved toward Knight's office with the inspector following, but when I rose to trail along, Isobel said, 'Can you spare a minute, Manny?'

Stopping, I said, 'Sure.'

Fausta asked sweetly, 'Want me to step outside?'

'That won't be necessary,' Isobel said in an equally sweet tone. 'Manny and I have already covered all we need to say to each other in private.'

Fausta's eyes developed a glitter that decided me to move my good shin out of kicking range. I went back to my chair.

Isobel asked me, 'Why did you think it funny I did not mention the grieving widow was closeted with my husband and his lawyer?'

'I didn't think it funny. I merely commented.'

'You said thin walls. Do you know what they were talking about?'

'Yes.'

When I failed to elaborate, she asked, 'Well, what?'

'Why?'

She bit her lip, glanced sidewise at Fausta and said, 'Has it anything to do with what we were discussing the other day?'

Suddenly I saw the light. She was afraid her husband and Mrs. Knight were comparing notes about Willard Knight's 'board meetings,' and with her husband's lawyer in on the conference, naturally she was upset.

Rising, I said, 'Relax, Isobel. They're discussing what Mrs. Knight should receive for her husband's share of the business. Apparently your husband wants to buy her out.'

She looked surprised. 'But the funeral hasn't even been held yet! It's not until tomorrow.' Then her expression turned scornful. 'She was always an unfeeling woman. Not a drop of sympathy or understanding in her veins. No wonder Willard searched elsewhere . . . ' Abruptly she stopped and glanced at Fausta again.

I said in a bored tone, 'I know. His wife didn't understand him.'

I was moving toward the room containing the inspector and Harlan Jones when Isobel said to my back, 'Well, she didn't. She didn't even show sympathy when she learned Willard was facing ruin because of what that Mr. Lancaster had found out, and might even have to go to jail. She just berated him for borrowing the money.'

My hand was on the knob of Knight's office door before Isobel's remark completely penetrated. Releasing the knob, I retraced my steps and sat down again.

To Fausta I said, 'Isobel and I have some more confidential things to say to each other. Go talk to Miss Graves.'

Curiously Fausta examined the expression on my face, decided it was no time for games, and followed orders without even her usual pretense of jealousy.

When she was out of earshot, I said,

'Now just repeat that last remark, Isobel.'

'About Willard's wife bawling him out?'

I nodded.

Isobel looked puzzled. 'She just bawled him out, that's all.'

'For borrowing money to speculate?'

'Well, for getting caught at it. Personally I think she wouldn't even have objected if Willard had made a killing. She was just mad over the jam he was in, not about the moral issue.'

'I see,' I said. 'And when did this bawling-out take place?'

'The evening he was at my house. That is, just before he got to my house. Willard told me he made a clean breast of everything when he got home from work, and she raised so much Cain, he told her he had a board meeting and walked out without even eating dinner.'

'He told her everything?' I asked carefully. 'About borrowing seventy thousand dollars to buy Ilco Utilities, about Lancaster threatening to knock the props from under Ilco with his public announcement, and about his argument with Lancaster?'

'Well,' she hedged, 'he told her all

about the jam he was in. He didn't tell *me* the details. I learned them since from Harlan and you. Willard just told me he was in a stock-market jam, had told his wife the whole story, and instead of trying to be helpful, she jumped all over him. You can see from that what kind of woman she is. Had she been a halfway adequate wife, she would never have driven her husband to seek sympathy and understanding from another woman.'

Had Isobel's revelation not opened an entirely new avenue of exploration, I might have been amused by the self-righteous manner in which she criticized another woman's marital sufficiency. But my mind was too busy to linger over pot-and-kettle philosophy. I said, 'Pardon me,' rose, and went into Willard Knight's office.

I found the inspector and Jones craning over a typed sheet lying on the desk between them. The inspector was listening without much interest as Jones explained each item listed on the sheet. I gathered it was a complete list of Willard Knight's borrowings, with dates of both the borrowings and returns, and amounts involved.

I interrupted to say, 'Let that ride awhile, Inspector. I just uncovered something more urgent.'

Day looked up at me with a scowl.

Conscious of the thin partition that would allow Mrs. Knight in the other office to hear every word I said in a normal tone, I moved close to the inspector and dropped my voice to a near whisper. 'Remember what a point Mrs. Knight made of not knowing what her husband saw in the paper? I just learned she knew all about Knight's jam, including his argument with Lancaster.'

The inspector's scowl faded to a blank look. 'How'd you find that out?'

I opened my mouth to explain, then suddenly realized I couldn't in front of Jones without disclosing that while he was in Kansas City, Isobel and Knight had spent the evening together.

'Something Fausta happened to say,' I improvised. 'I'll explain it later. Since Mrs. Knight is right next door, suppose we ask her a few questions.'

Jones said, 'You mean interrupt our conference?' and when the inspector merely gave him an irritated look, hastily added, 'Not that I mind for myself. But my lawyer is a busy man and — '

'So am I,' Day said bluntly. 'Moon, bring that woman in here.'

'Sure, Inspector.' I started for the door, stopped again, and asked Jones, 'Whose idea was this conference between you and Mrs. Knight?'

Jones looked puzzled. 'What do you mean?'

I said, 'A little while ago I stepped in here to borrow a chair. Your walls aren't very thick and I couldn't help overhearing the discussion next door. It struck me the division of the business was being somewhat rushed inasmuch as your partner hasn't even been buried yet. I just wondered who was doing the rushing.'

'I see,' Jones said slowly. 'It is a trifle untimely, isn't it? But Mrs. Knight insisted. I certainly am in no hurry. As a matter of fact I would prefer some delay, as I am going to have to borrow a good portion of what it will take to buy her out.

I understand she is in a hurry because she plans to leave town immediately after the funeral. She mentioned something about living with a sister in California.'

22

I think Harlan Jones's lawyer intended to wax a little pompous about his time being valuable when we intruded on his conference, but one snarl from Warren Day decided him not even to open his mouth. With a definite lead to follow, the inspector became overbearingly dictatorial. He not only cowed the lawyer into submission, he high-handedly ordered Harlan Jones to stay out of his own office while Mrs. Knight was being questioned, apparently to forestall possible eavesdropping through the thin partition.

Denied access to his work sanctum, Harlan decided to leave the office temporarily with his wife and his lawyer. From the ruffled appearances of the two men, I suspect they headed for the nearest bar.

Leaving Fausta in the company of Matilda Graves, we ushered Mrs. Knight into her deceased husband's office and closed the door. The inspector ensconced himself behind the dead man's desk, summarily waved the widow into the lone remaining guest chair, and left me standing.

After getting the woman in the proper mood for a confidential chat by glaring at her silently and ferociously for nearly a minute, Day suddenly said in a silky voice, 'Understand you're planning to leave town, Mrs. Knight.'

Had he possessed a sleek black mustache to twirl, hissed his words and called her 'my proud beauty' instead of 'Mrs. Knight,' he could have given no more perfect a portrayal of a villain about to foreclose the mortgage. The woman stared at him in bewilderment.

'Why, yes, after the funeral,' she said finally. 'I plan to live with a sister in California. With Willard gone, there is nothing to hold me here.'

The inspector nodded with sinister satisfaction. In the same cat-and-mouse tone, he said, 'As I recall your statement, you had no idea at the time why your husband disappeared after the Lancaster murder.'

She looked even more bewildered. 'That's right, Inspector. Of course now I realize it was because he knew he would be suspected of the murder. But I'm sure Willard was innocent.'

'So am I,' Day said agreeably. Abruptly he shot at me, 'Moon, tell Mrs. Knight what you just learned.'

'Sure, Inspector. Mrs. Knight, when I first talked to you, and later when you gave a formal statement to the police, you made a great point of your ignorance of your husband's affairs. As I recall, prior to my visit you had no idea what it was he saw in the newspaper that upset him so much.'

Her husky voice seemed to me to grow an edge of caution. 'I thought it probably was something on the market page.'

'It never even occurred to you it might have been the Lancaster killing?'

After a nearly imperceptible pause, she said, 'Of course not.'

'That's odd,' I remarked. 'You must have forgotten that only the evening before your husband told you all about his predicament, including his argument with Walter Lancaster.'

Her face continued to look only puzzled, but I was watching her hands, and they suddenly clenched together so tightly, the knuckles turned white. 'He didn't mention Mr. Lancaster. He only — ' Abruptly she stopped, then proceeded in a more even tone, 'I don't know why you men think you have to trap me into something or other with trick questions. You couldn't possibly know what my husband said to me in private.'

'Your husband repeated it, Mrs. Knight. He told the whole story of your domestic squabble to a drinking companion while he was supposed to be at his 'board meeting.' We have the evidence of the drinking companion.'

For a long time she made no comment. Her hands worked together as though she were kneading dough, and her face assumed a pinched, angry expression.

Finally she said in a furious voice, 'That woman! You say drinking companion, but loving companion is more like it! He told that skinny redheaded thing!'

'Oh, so you knew he was having an

affair with Mrs. Jones?'

'Mrs. Whore is more like it,' she said hysterically. 'Snatching other women's husbands when she's got a perfectly good man of her own.' Then she seemed to realize she was reacting exactly as we wished, and sullenly drew her lips into a thin line.

I asked, 'If you knew your husband was seeing Mrs. Jones, how does it happen you never compared notes with Mr. Jones? You don't impress me as a woman who would accept a situation like that without some action.'

Her lips began to tremble, and suspecting she was going to cry, Warren Day glared at her so belligerently she was startled into changing her mind. Just being in the same room with a woman was trial enough for the inspector. A weeping woman was more than he intended to bear.

'I did try to talk to him about two months ago,' she said in a shaky voice. 'But she's got him so fooled, he's stark blind. He said women my age sometimes begin imagining things about their husbands, and he was sure when my period of adjustment was over, I'd realize Willard was a good husband. I guess Willard had told him I was beginning to have female trouble, and he thought my suspicions were just part of the sickness. His talking down to me like he was a doctor or something made me so furious, I never mentioned it to him again.'

The inspector cleared his throat as a signal to me he was ready to take over. I leaned against the wall and waited.

He had decided to drop the silkily villainous approach in favor of impersonal brusqueness. 'We've strayed from the original point a little, Mrs. Knight. It's useless for you to deny your husband told you all about the scrape he was in the evening Lancaster was killed, and you deliberately concealed that fact from the police.'

Her head gave a frightened shake. 'Not all, he didn't tell me. Just that he'd borrowed a lot of money to invest in stock, and one of the other stockholders was going to let it out the next morning that the stock had a false value. He said he was ruined and might even go to jail, but he never told me who the man was who was causing all the trouble. He never mentioned Mr. Lancaster's name.'

Without belief Day asked, 'Then why did you deny knowing anything about your husband's affairs?'

'Willard told me to. I lied about what happened the next morning too, but I had to. When he saw the headline about Mr. Lancaster's murder, he told me he was the man who had intended to ruin him. He said he could dispose of the bad stock if he had twenty-four hours, and if the police came I should stall them off to give him time. What else could I do? I didn't want Willard to be ruined and have to go to prison.'

The inspector said dryly, 'This is the second plausible story you've told, Mrs. Knight. First you know nothing about your husband's stock-market jam, then when you get caught in the lie, you suddenly know half the details. Just enough to explain the lie, but not enough to make it possible that *you* killed Walter Lancaster.'

The woman's eyes widened with a

mixture of astonishment and indignation.

But before she could speak, the inspector hammered at her, 'I think your husband told you the full story, including the name of the man who was going to ruin him and the information that he was dining at El Patio that night. And after your husband left the house, I think you drove out to El Patio, hid in the bushes and shot Walter Lancaster in order to save your husband from ruin.'

'Why, we don't even own a car!' Mrs. Knight said indignantly. 'Nor a gun either.'

Momentarily the inspector looked disconcerted. Then brushing the objection aside with the remark that cars are easily rented, he drove straight on, ticking each point off on his fingers as he made it.

'First, your motive for killing Lancaster was as great as your husband's. If Knight crashed financially, you crashed right along with him. Second, you had opportunity while your husband was at his 'board meeting.' Only your unsupported story puts you home all evening. Third — '

Mrs. Knight's mannish voice abruptly interrupted him. 'I thought the same person who killed Mr. Lancaster killed Willard too. Am I supposed to have saved Willard by murder one day, and killed him the next?'

'Exactly,' the inspector said with relish. Drawing on his vast knowledge of feminine psychology, which totaled zero, he explained. 'I imagine you loved your husband, and women are always shooting the men they love. In Homicide we never get a case of a woman shooting some man she doesn't like. It's always the guy she loves. You loved Knight enough to kill for him, so naturally you loved him enough to kill him. The age-old motive of jealousy. He was out with Mrs. Jones the night he got it.'

Gently I thrust a thought into the discussion. 'How about the attempt on Fausta, Inspector? That was by a man.'

Day turned to glare at me, thought a moment, and suddenly looked happy again. 'Listen to her voice,' he said. 'Imagine it coming over a telephone.'

Thoughtfully I examined the woman, who gradually seemed to be nearing the bursting point. 'You mean it could pass for a man's? Possibly. It's pretty deep and husky.'

Mrs. Knight reached her bursting point. 'I never heard anything so ridiculous in my life!' she half-shouted. 'Accusing me of killing my own husband, plus a man I didn't even know! You'd do better out on the street looking for real murderers than trying to scare an innocent woman.'

Both of us merely looked at her until her anger deflated. Then she said in a small voice, 'Besides, even if I could imitate a man's voice over the phone, I couldn't have passed for a man in a barroom. It was a man who ordered that drink for Miss Moreni.'

The inspector pounced. 'How do you know what almost happened to Miss Moreni, Mrs. Knight?'

She looked confused. 'It was in the paper.'

Slowly the inspector shook his head.

'On the radio then.'

Again there was a slow headshake. 'It was deliberately kept out. Only the waiter's death was reported.'

Much as it pained me, I was forced to

destroy his beautiful dream. 'Don Bell had it on his broadcast last night, Inspector. So it's probably in the morning papers too. I haven't seen them.'

Apparently neither had the inspector. He glared at me. Just before he burst, I said reasonably, 'I didn't give Bell the item, Inspector. And you've still got a pretty good case against Mrs. Knight.'

For a few moments Day did not trust himself to speak. Finally he rose from his chair and said in a strangled voice, 'I think we'll continue this downtown, Mrs. Knight. You are under arrest on suspicion of homicide.'

The woman made no objection whatever, but I got the impression this was not a tacit admission of guilt, but simply the result of not knowing what to do about the matter. As the inspector started to lead her out, it occurred to me his logical case might fall apart from lack of proof unless he got a confession.

I stopped him by asking, 'Think you've got it solved finally, Inspector?'

He swung about to stare at me with suspicion. 'Don't you, Moon?'

I shrugged. 'I haven't the faintest idea. It's a nice logical case, but it does have the weak point Mrs. Knight mentioned. It *was* a man who ordered that drink for Fausta.'

Irritably he glanced from me to Mrs. Knight, who sullenly waited beside him, then back at me again. 'Or a woman in man's clothes. For that matter, who said it was a man? The only person who saw the poisoner was the waiter, and he's dead. Also, poison is a woman's weapon.'

I grinned at him. 'That's an old wives' tale. At least half the famous poisoners in history were men.'

'And at least half the famous women in history were poisoners,' he snapped back, allowing his opinion of womanhood in general to shade his recollection of history.

I said, 'Just remember our agreement, Inspector. Twenty-four hours.'

He gave me a sour look, but nodded his head. 'It'll be at least that before we're ready to lodge a formal charge anyway.' Turning to his prisoner, he said, 'Let's go, lady.'

Since we had come in my car, Fausta and I dropped Day and Mrs. Knight at headquarters, then proceeded on to the nearest bar, where Fausta had a plain Coke, but I, lacking her prejudice against drinking before lunch, ordered a rye and water.

When over our drinks I had explained developments to Fausta, she asked, 'You think perhaps I am in no more danger then?'

'You'll continue to have me around as a bodyguard until they get a confession out of Mrs. Knight,' I told her. 'There's a better case against her than any we've had yet, but I don't like her reaction.'

'How do you mean, Manny?'

'She's not scared enough. Oh, she's scared all right, but no more than any innocent person might be when suddenly accused of murder. And she exhibits just the right amount of indignation. I don't think she's smart enough to put on a good act, and if she were acting, I have a feeling she'd overdo the indignation.'

'Then you think she isn't the killer after all?'

I shrugged. 'I didn't say that. I just said

I'm not letting you out of my sight until we're sure.'

It occurred to me I had not yet made my promised call to Laurie Davis, and now was as good a time as any. From the barroom booth I called the private number in Carson City Davis had given me, but it was a wasted thirty-five cents. The male secretary who answered sounded surprised when he learned who was calling.

'I thought Mr. Davis was with you,' he said. 'He left your number to call in case I needed him.'

Hanging up, I phoned Murdoch, the manager of the apartment house where I live.

'Yes, Mr. Moon,' he told me. 'Mr. Davis and a friend are here now. I recognized Mr. Davis from his news pictures and took the liberty of letting them in your apartment to wait. Was that all right?'

'Quite,' I said. 'Mind telling Mr. Davis to hang on and I'll be there in ten minutes?'

Murdoch said he didn't mind.

23

We found Laurie Davis and Farmer Cole quietly waiting in my front room. They were better behaved than my usual run of guests, neither having his feet on my cocktail table as one of the previous night's callers had, and neither having taken the liberty of sampling my rye.

I offered some of the latter item, but got polite refusals from both. Beyond a friendly but formal greeting to Fausta, Laurie Davis paid no attention to her, his mind apparently being strictly on business.

'I had expected to hear from you before now, Mr. Moon,' he started mildly.

I told him I had just called his private number in Carson City, which was how I had learned he was here.

'I'm not used to chasing after the people I hire,' he commented heavily, but still in a mild enough voice.

'I figured you were getting regular reports on my activities from the Farmer,'

I said with equal mildness. 'I was afraid if I duplicated his efforts, he might end up out of a job.'

Farmer Cole turned his flat eyes toward me, and Laurie said without humor, 'You two seem to rub against each other. If you tried to get better acquainted, I have an idea you'd find you have a lot in common.'

The suggestion stirred no emotions whatever in my heart, and the Farmer's expression indicated the thought pained him.

Davis, as on his previous visit, occupied my favorite chair, his big body relaxed to the point of inertia and his sleepy eyes half-shut. He asked slowly, 'Have you made any substantial progress?'

'Possibly,' I said. 'Warren Day has made an arrest, but I'm not certain he has Lancaster's killer. It's Mrs. Knight, Willard Knight's widow.'

'Oh? And her supposed motive?'

'Willard Knight had been playing the stock market with company funds. Walter Lancaster threatened to make public certain irregularities in a corporation where Knight owned seventy thousand dollars' worth of stock. Mrs. Knight knew all about it, and the theory is she bumped Lancaster to save her husband from bankruptcy and prison, then bumped her husband because he was playing another woman.'

In a sleepy sort of way the big man looked pleased with me for some reason. 'But you're not enthusiastic about this theory?'

'I'm not unenthusiastic about it. I've still got an open mind. I think it's quite probable the motive for murdering Lancaster was to prevent his making his knowledge public, but any number of people may have had that motive.'

Laurie's eyes were almost drooping shut as he asked idly, 'What was the name of this precarious corporation?'

As though I had not heard the question, I said, 'Knight may have been killed for the same reason your lieutenant governor was, the killer assuming he was the only person aside from Lancaster who knew the corporation was unsound.'

The big man let his eyes open halfway. 'And who would be the killer with that motive?'

'Whoever was responsible for the

corporation's fix. Maybe a member of the board of directors.'

When no one said anything for a few moments, I added brightly, 'You're on all sorts of corporation boards, aren't you, Mr. Davis?'

The closest thing to a smile he had yet managed in my presence appeared on Laurie Davis's face. It was not actually a smile, for that would have required too strenuous use of his facial muscles, but it definitely was an expression of amusement. He looked over at Fausta.

'Your friend fully comes up to your recommendation, Fausta. I'm glad I hired him.' Then his eyes swung back to me. 'You consider all possible suspects, don't you, Mr. Moon? Including your own client.'

'The possibility occurred to me,' I admitted. 'Though now I'm inclined to scratch you off my list of suspects.'

'Thank you,' he said dryly. 'What did you say the name of this corporation was?'

'I didn't say, Mr. Davis. The reason I've scratched you as a suspect is that I've figured out why you hired me. And it wasn't quite the reason you gave.'

Heavy-lidded eyes centered on my face, but he made no comment.

'You didn't actually fear any political scandal in connection with Walter Lancaster's death,' I said. 'The guy was so honest, there wasn't a chance in a million he'd be tied up with anything unsavory. You did suspect he might have been killed to shut him up about a financial swindle he'd uncovered, however, and you weren't sure just how that swindle might affect your own finances.'

I waited a moment for verification, but when none was forthcoming, went on. 'Apparently Lancaster's motive in calling on Knight before he made his public disclosure was to justify his action to his old college chum. From what Knight's secretary overheard of the conversation, Knight tried to blame Lancaster for getting him involved in the company. Lancaster hadn't recommended the stock, and seemingly had a clear conscience insofar as Knight's jam was concerned, but they had discussed the stock previously, and apparently Lancaster anticipated Knight might blame him. Obviously he had no intention of giving Knight a special break, so his visit must have been inspired by the hope he could convince his friend of the rightness of his decision in advance of the announcement, and save their friendship. I suppose he thought there would be a better chance of this if he told Knight what he intended to do in advance, rather than letting him read it in the papers.'

Laurie Davis seemed to be going to sleep. I stopped talking, and after a moment his eyes opened and he looked at me as though wondering why I had stopped. Seeing I had not lost his attention, I continued.

'I'm going to make a guess that Lancaster afforded you the same treatment he did Knight,' I said. 'Only when he told you, there was still plenty of time to dump your shares. I'm guessing that he told you only that he'd uncovered a swindle, but refused to tell you what company was involved, because he didn't want you to dump your shares. He was so honest, he refused to let even close friends have any advantage over the rest of the stockholders, but at the same time he wanted his friends to understand he was acting because his conscience would let him act in no other way, and not simply acting in callous disregard to their welfare. What I don't understand is why you simply didn't dump all the stock you owned in the five companies Lancaster had an interest in. One of the five had to be it.'

'Because that would have started a general panic,' Davis said simply. 'I had twenty-seven other corporations to consider.'

After thinking this over for a short time, I thought I understood what he meant. His business interests were so vast and complicated, his sudden retreat from five corporations all at once might have created an impression with the public that the whole financial structure was tumbling. And at the very least this would have caused decided stock-market fluctuations. Whereas dumping his interest in a single corporation would have no such effect.

'I see,' I said. 'You had to know exactly what stock it was that had a phony value, so you could quietly get out from under and let the small stockholders take the rap. It was such a delicate situation, you couldn't afford even a rumor until you knew for certain why Lancaster had been killed. You gave me a cock-and-bull story about needing twenty-four hours to repair political fences, and hired me to unearth the motive for the killing. If the motive proved to be something other than you suspected, no harm was done. But if it was to shut Lancaster up because of a stock swindle, the public disclosure of which would knock the bottom out of the stock, you wanted a twenty-four-hour jump on everybody else.'

When I stopped speaking, there was silence in the room for several minutes. Finally Laurie said, 'So?'

'So I think it's a shame a guy as honest as Walter Lancaster should die for nothing. I have an idea he was thinking of the little stockholders when he refused to take advantage of his knowledge to save his own investment or the investments of other large stockholders. People who had their life savings tied up in this corporation. Call me a damn fool idealist if you want, but like Walter, I'm a champion of the little guy. You're going to learn the name of the shaky corporation when you read it in the newspapers.'

Laurie's sleepy eyes became bare slits. 'You accepted a retainer to carry out specific instructions, Mr. Moon. And there was nothing illegal about what I hired you to do.'

'Nothing illegal,' I admitted. 'I'll give you an argument about your ethics though. Anyway, you've got your facts twisted. I accepted a retainer to investigate a case, and you promised an additional thousand dollars if I delivered certain information to you twenty-four hours before the public got it. My failure to deliver automatically releases you from your part of the bargain.'

Slowly he moved his head back and forth. 'I'm afraid I can't accept that, Mr. Moon.'

'I'm afraid there's nothing else you can do, Mr. Davis.'

'Oh, but there is,' he assured me. He glanced at Farmer Cole, then at Fausta and back to me. 'I understand Miss

Moreni had an attempt made on her life, and you've appointed yourself her full-time bodyguard. Since you've decided I'm not a suspect, would you trust her with me if we went no further than the apartment manager's flat?'

I looked at him blankly. 'Why?'

'The Farmer wants to talk to you privately. It would be pleasanter for all concerned if Miss Moreni weren't here.'

Fausta looked from one to the other of us suspiciously. 'What is it, Manny?' she asked.

'Mr. Davis wants to find out if Farmer Cole and I actually do have anything in common,' I explained. 'Go along with Mr. Davis.'

She continued to sit. 'I do not like this,' she said determinedly. 'You are all acting funny. I will stay right here.'

'Do what I tell you!' I snapped at her.

Fausta's eyes widened. Ordinarily when you snap at Fausta, it is a good idea immediately to duck, but one look at my face dissuaded her from hurling any ashtrays.

Fausta is one of those rare women who

are used to having their way, but instantly recognize when a man cannot be pushed. She rose without further protest, gave me a troubled look and moved to the door.

Laurie escorted her out as courteously as though he were leading her onto a dance floor. At the door he paused to look back at me with no rancor whatever.

'Understand I have no quarrel with your ideals, Mr. Moon. As a matter of fact I admire a man with principles. It's one of the things which made me back Walter Lancaster for lieutenant governor. But if you insist on tweaking the devil's nose, you really have no cause for complaint when you find his horns in your stomach.'

'Sure,' I said dryly. 'No hard feelings. I'll ring Murdoch's flat when I'm ready for you to come after your boy.'

I think he might have let himself laugh had it not required so much effort. Instead he contented himself with a dry final remark.

'Let the Farmer call me, if you don't feel like lifting the phone.'

After the door closed, Farmer Cole and

I sat examining each other a few moments. Finally the Farmer spoke. 'All the boss wants is the name of that firm,' he said reasonably. 'You could save us both trouble.'

'You get paid pretty well?' I asked.

He considered the question. 'Pretty well.'

'Then why should I save you trouble? Earn your money.'

Still seated, he contemplated me with an almost vacuous expression on his face. Unexpectedly his hand flashed under his coat. On top of catching me completely by surprise, it was the fastest draw I ever saw, at least twice as fast as I could have managed. My fingers were just dipping past my lapel when I froze them there because I found myself staring at the bore of a forty-five automatic.

'I didn't expect gunplay,' I said. 'Going to shoot the information out of me?'

'The element of surprise is half the battle, son. Bring it out easy, with just your thumb and forefinger. Put it on the floor in front of you.'

In slow motion I complied.

'Now kick it over here.'

I toed the P-38 across to him.

Rising from his chair, he walked to the window in back of him and laid both guns on the sill. 'No gunplay,' he said explanatorily. 'Just a precaution. I couldn't have you reaching for a gun, and maybe have to wing you.'

'I see,' I said. 'Thoughtful of you.'

'Now the program,' he explained without expression, 'is for me to make you want to tell the name of that firm. It's only fair to tell you I know a million techniques, and you couldn't stop any of them. You got a last chance to tell me peacefully.'

'Stop calling it a firm,' I said. 'It's a corporation.'

Again he moved with the speed of light, but this time not unexpectedly. He intended it to be unexpected, but I have a prejudice against being caught napping twice in a row.

With almost unbelievable swiftness he was across the room and one bony hand was darting for my left wrist for a judo hold. I got the wrist out of the way by shooting a left jab where his face should have been.

It wasn't.

During the next few minutes I discovered the Farmer had better than an amateur knowledge of boxing, judo and plain wrestling. I have better than an amateur knowledge of the first two myself, having been a pro fighter and, for a short time, an army judo instructor. I even know the rudiments of wrestling.

In technical knowledge I considerably outclassed the ex-FBI man, but two factors more than counter balanced this advantage. The Farmer's lanky frame was encased in solid muscle which seemed to be interlaced with piano wire, and he could move faster than anyone I ever before even heard of.

Having felt his punch once before, I knew he had power as well as speed. But he made no attempt to hit me, employing his boxing skill only in defense. Apparently his design was to get me in his hands and bend parts of me until I felt like talking.

He would have been an infuriating ring opponent even for a champion, for his incredible speed made it impossible to hit him. Once I had a reputation for being fast in the ring, and in spite of a false leg, I still possess most of my co-ordination. Yet every blow I threw at him either met empty air, or slid harmlessly off his forearms. The closest I came to tagging him was a solid right cross meant for his jaw which landed high on his left shoulder.

The blow sent him staggering backward without hurting him in the least, but before I could follow it up, he skipped to one side, stopped out of range and gawked at me solemnly. Glad of the rest, I stopped too and listened to myself pant.

'You're good,' he said with faint admiration. 'That one almost nailed me.'

Since getting my breath seemed more important than verbal badinage, I refrained from replying.

'Shall we try an encore?' he asked, suddenly darting in again.

During the brief respite I had decided it was futile to wear myself out swinging at a phantom. If he wanted judo, we would fight on his terms awhile and see what happened.

What happened was that he threw me

half across the room on my face, flopped on my back before I could roll clear, clamped a scissors around my legs and twisted my right arm up into the middle of my back, where he kept it with a double arm lock.

'In case you hadn't noticed, the fight is over,' he said.

Gradually he increased the pressure on my arm. When he saw the sweat dripping from my face and knew the pain almost had me screaming, he said, 'This goes on until you tell me that firm's name.'

You don't stand pain like that for long without either crying uncle or going unconscious, and he kept it at a point just short of where I could find relief in unconsciousness. He kept it there for five minutes.

'You're biting your lip,' he said finally. 'It's bleeding.'

I decided to break the hold.

On television, wrestlers break holds even more complicated than a combination scissors and double-arm lock, but you rarely see it done in an amateur match. There it usually ends the fight.

Possibly a professional could have squirmed out of the hold without personal damage, but the only way I knew how to do it involved deliberately dislocating my own shoulder.

Working my left hand under my chest, I began to draw my knees forward.

'You damn fool!' the Farmer said. 'Don't make me cripple you.'

Slowly, despite the excruciating pain, I forced my knees forward until they were solidly under me. The next step was to push my face off the floor, roll sidewise and dislocate my shoulder.

Farmer Cole knew exactly what I was doing. When I got my face six inches from the floor, he suddenly released me.

When I climbed unsteadily to my feet and began to massage my numb arm, he was standing three feet away eying me moodily.

'I pass,' he said.

I continued to massage my arm.

'I shouldn't waste my time,' he elaborated. 'Any idiot stubborn enough to pull what you just tried isn't going to tell me anything no matter what I do to him.'

'That's right,' I agreed. Licking my lips, I discovered he had been telling the truth about my biting them. They tasted of blood.

'So it's a draw,' the Farmer said. 'No hard feelings?'

'No hard feelings,' I told him.

Then *I* moved unexpectedly for a change. Driving forward, I wrapped him in a bear hug and carried him against the wall at a dead run. As the air whooshed out of him, I banged him in the left eye with my forehead. That dazed him enough so that he stood still while I unwrapped my arms and smashed an elbow into his jaw. I followed it with the other elbow, stepped back and watched him slide to a sitting position on the floor.

His jaw must have been iron, for he wasn't quite out even after that punishment. After a moment he shook his head and looked at me groggily.

'The element of surprise is half the battle, son,' I told him.

The damned fool grinned at me.

24

It was another twenty minutes before we bothered to phone Murdoch's apartment. First we brushed each other off, then washed our hands and faces, then he painted my lip with iodine and I put a cold compress on his left eye. After that we had a drink.

By the time the Farmer finally got around to phoning, we were on our second drink and had discovered, as Laurie Davis suggested, we had a lot in common. I was mixing a third drink when Laurie and Fausta returned.

Both of them looked from my swollen lip to the Farmer's swollen eye, but neither said anything.

'It was a draw,' Farmer Cole explained briefly.

I mixed drinks for Fausta and Davis.

I have to credit Laurie Davis with being a cheerful loser. He simply accepted the situation and asked no questions whatever. His sole reference to the matter was an oblique remark he made just as he and the Farmer were leaving.

'If the Farmer ever leaves me, would you be interested in a job as a bodyguard, Mr. Moon?' he asked.

'Let's take that up when it happens,' I suggested.

When they were gone, Fausta said, 'I never in my life heard of such childishness. Two grown men fighting like babies, and then ending up friends. Your lip looks awful.'

I grinned at her.

'Also, it is way after noon, and time for you to feed me.'

Since she wanted to check up on how the club was functioning in her absence, we killed two birds with one stone by lunching at El Patio. It was a casual remark of Fausta's during lunch which upset the applecart of the assassin of Walter Lancaster and Willard Knight. She said, 'Does it not make you think sometimes, Manny, that a person's whole life may be changed by some small irrelevant thing which in itself is entirely unrelated to the person?'

Having just finished dessert, I was feeling unsuccessfully for a cigar. As I signaled a nearby cigarette girl, I said, 'You mean, for instance, had there been a cigar in my pocket, probably I would never have noticed the shapely brunette approaching? But because of the irrelevant fact that I am out of cigars at this precise instant, perhaps we shall accidentally look into each other's eyes, and ten years from now we'll be the fond parents of eight children.'

'If you raise your eyes above her tray,' Fausta said firmly, 'I will fire her on the spot.'

I disregarded her instructions, but nothing happened. She was just another pretty girl, and I was just another customer to her.

As I lighted my cigar, Fausta said, 'What I was thinking of was this morning. Had there been one more chair in the Jones and Knight office, Mrs. Knight would not have been arrested for murder.'

'You've got your small, irrelevant things twisted,' I said. 'It was an idle remark by Isobel Jones which set us after Mrs. Knight.'

'Yes, but if you had not gone into Willard Knight's office after a chair, you would not have heard Mrs. Knight in the next office, so would not have mentioned her when you came out. Then Mrs. Jones would have had no occasion to make the remark.'

'I suppose so,' I said without much interest. The school of philosophy which holds our lives are conditioned largely by minor and random events has never appealed to me much.

Nevertheless, Fausta's remark started me thinking about the incident, and almost unobtrusively a thought floated into my mind which pointed a finger of suspicion in an entirely new direction. The more I thought about it, and the more I related it to previous minor details which had come up during the investigation, the surer I became that I finally knew the real killer.

Fausta asked, 'What is the matter with you, Manny? All at once you look as if you are in a daze.'

'I want to make some phone calls from your office,' I said, rising abruptly. 'Come along.'

My first call was to the airport, and my second to the office of the Jones and Knight Investment Company. Matilda Graves informed me Harlan Jones had never returned to the office after Day drove him from his room. He had called from home to tell her he was taking the day off, and I could probably reach him there.

My third call was to Warren Day at headquarters. When he heard what I had to say, he didn't even put up an argument. 'Meet you in front of the house in fifteen minutes,' he said, and hung up.

We timed it just right, swinging in behind the squad car just as it stopped at the curb. As the inspector stepped from the right-hand door, Hannegan got out from the driver's side. Fausta and I trailed them up the walk to the front porch.

In deference to the heat both Isobel and her husband were attired in sports clothes and were enjoying the relative coolness of the front porch. Isobel, as usual, looked better for being largely exposed, but Harlan's orange shorts and thin T-shirt only succeeded in making him incongruous. He had too little chest, too much stomach and too-hairy legs for the combination.

Isobel merely smiled us a languid greeting, but Harlan fought his way out of his nearly horizontal deck chair and began trying to figure out where on the porch to seat four more people. Aside from the deck chairs he and his wife were occupying, the porch contained only a swing and one canvas chair.

'Sit down and stop fluttering,' Isobel told him. 'They'll find places to sit.'

Seating herself in the porch swing, Fausta looked at the inspector and patted the place beside her. He favored her with a look of utter astonishment and firmly seated himself on the broad railing. I decided to keep Fausta company and Hannegan silently lowered himself into the chair.

'Go mix some drinks, Harlan,' Isobel suggested.

The inspector shook his head. 'I have to inform you this is an official visit.'

'More questions?' Isobel asked. 'I thought after you arrested the widow, it was all over.'

'Something new has come up,' the inspector said heavily. He looked at Harlan Jones and bluntly asked, 'Where were you the evening Walter Lancaster was killed?'

The little fat man stared at him blankly. 'Why, in Kansas City. I told you that.'

Day shook his head. 'A little while ago, Moon phoned the airport. There was no reservation in your name Monday night.'

Isobel said in a surprised tone, 'You just now checked up? I thought the first thing the police did was check alibis.'

Day's face grew a deep red. When he opened his mouth to speak, nothing came out but an unintelligible sputter.

I went to his rescue. 'It was a silly oversight on my part as well as on the part of the police. But your husband wasn't suspected of anything, and after both his secretary and his wife told us he had flown to Kansas City, it just never occurred to anyone to check up. Since we were satisfied Walter Lancaster's sole connection with the Jones and Knight Company had been his dealings with Willard Knight, and your husband had neither any business nor social connections with the man, there wasn't any reason to suspect him.'

Isobel turned to her husband. 'Where were you, Harlan?' Then an expression of incredulity grew on her face. 'Harlan! You couldn't possibly have another woman!'

Harlan merely looked at her piteously and licked his lips.

'No, he hasn't another woman,' I told her. 'But he knew you had another man. He knew if he let it be known he was flying out of town, the minute his plane was supposed to leave, Willard Knight would be over here.'

Isobel said indignantly, 'Manny Moon! You promised me — '

'I'm not saying anything he doesn't know,' I assured her. 'He's known about you and Knight for at least two months. Mrs. Knight told him. That's how he knew Knight would be here at the time Lancaster was killed, making Knight a perfect alibi, but one he couldn't use.'

Isobel looked from me to her husband and back again. 'I don't understand. You can't possibly mean Harlan is a murderer.'

Her puzzlement was natural, for I have

never seen anyone who looked less like a killer than the crushed little man in his ridiculous orange shorts and T-shirt.

'I'm afraid he is,' I said gently. 'He had exactly the same motive we attributed to Mrs. Knight. It was there for us all the time, but Harlan's timorousness made us overlook him as a possibility. Maybe it was that timorousness which sent him over the line. Maybe he couldn't stand the thought of facing ruin, which was what he visualized when he overheard your lover and Lancaster arguing on the other side of that thin partition, and realized Knight's financial loss would bankrupt the firm.

'He knew how his partner would react to Lancaster's death, knew the moment he learned of it, he would unload the stock and return the money to the company account. He must have planned it all out while listening to Knight and Lancaster argue. In the middle of the argument he went next door, ostensibly to quiet Knight down, and surreptitiously opened the key of Knight's call box. This allowed Matilda Graves to hear the tail end of the argument, thereby establishing a witness to Knight's threat. Then he went home, established an alibi for himself by phoning back to the office and leaving word he was flying out of town, and at the same time put Knight in a position where he couldn't explain where he was when Lancaster was shot.'

Isobel looked at her husband with disbelief. When he did nothing but continue to look back at her piteously, she turned her attention back to me. 'But — but — ' she stuttered, 'why would he then kill Willard? If he put up with Willard and me for two months without even opening his mouth, why suddenly kill him?'

The inspector recovered his voice. 'Once you've killed, the second time is easy. The penalty for one murder is the same as the penalty for fifty.'

'Also,' I put in, 'perhaps Harlan felt stealing his wife was one thing, but when Knight started stealing his money, he was going too far.'

Warren Day stared at the little man until Harlan seemed to shrink into himself. 'Why don't you tell us about it?' he said in a surprisingly gentle voice.

Harlan's lips moved silently. Finally he got out, 'You seem to know everything.'

'Why did you decide to kill Knight?'

His lips moved again for a moment without sound, then he managed to say in a dejected tone, 'I followed Isobel to the Sheridan when she sneaked out to meet Willard, and through a window of the lounge I saw them together. When Willard suddenly entered the lobby, I went around to the hotel's main entrance and saw him waiting for an elevator. I took the stairs to the second floor and caught the same elevator on the way up. Willard was surprised to see me, but he gave no sign he knew me because he was there under an assumed name, you see, and I suppose he was afraid I would address him by his right name. He made a motion for me to follow, and when we got off the elevator we went to his room together without exchanging a word. After he had closed the door, he demanded to know why I was following him.'

The little man paused while his eyes

stared sightlessly in front of him, seeing not a group of people gathered on a cool front porch, but the interior of a hotel room.

'I didn't know exactly why I was following him, except that it seemed to be time for a showdown about Isobel. I had things to say about his embezzlement, of course, but I had checked with the bank before closing time and knew the money was safely back in our account, so that discussion could have waited until he returned to the office. I told him I wanted him to stay away from Isobel.'

Again he paused, and this time when he resumed, his voice was barely audible. 'He said he loved her, both he and she intended to get divorces, and he meant to marry her. And then he laughed at me.'

He stopped speaking, this time for good, letting us visualize the rest for ourselves. It was not hard: a round little fat man confronted by a tall, virile rival who had cheated him, stolen his beautiful wife, and now destroyed his dignity with the final insult of laughter. Momentarily I almost found myself sympathizing with him, but then I remembered he was the same killer who had attempted to murder Fausta.

Fausta remembered it at the same moment. Staring at Jones with the same fascination with which she might have regarded a freak in a side show, she said, 'Now I understand why you looked as if you were seeing a ghost the first time we met. You thought you had just poisoned me.'

'Yeah,' I said. 'He also thought you'd immediately recognize him as Lancaster's killer when you walked into his office with me, not knowing the story that you had seen his face was a deliberate plant.'

At a gesture from Warren Day, Hannegan heaved to his feet and curtly motioned for Jones to arise. Numbly the little man got up, then gazed down at his wife in mute appeal.

But Isobel was already regarding him as though he were something without much interest from her past. Her eyes flicked over him indifferently, then settled thoughtfully on the burly figure of Lieutenant Hannegan. You could almost see her filing him away in her mind as a future possibility to while away an evening of boredom. I had a feeling that if she had him alone for a moment, she would issue an invitation for that evening.

Suddenly she smiled brightly up at Harlan. 'I suppose you've it arranged for me to inherit everything, haven't you, dear?'

Fausta forgot she was a lady. Leaving her seat next to me almost as fast as Farmer Cole could have moved, she planted a beautiful roundhouse square in Isobel's lovely left eye.

We do hope that you have enjoyed reading this large print book.

Did you know that all of our titles are available for purchase?

We publish a wide range of high quality large print books including:
Romances, Mysteries, Classics
General Fiction
Non Fiction and Westerns

Special interest titles available in large print are:
The Little Oxford Dictionary
Music Book, Song Book
Hymn Book, Service Book

Also available from us courtesy of Oxford University Press:
Young Readers' Dictionary
(large print edition)
Young Readers' Thesaurus
(large print edition)

For further information or a free brochure, please contact us at:
Ulverscroft Large Print Books Ltd.,
The Green, Bradgate Road, Anstey,
Leicester, LE7 7FU, England.
Tel: (00 44) **0116 236 4325**
Fax: (00 44) **0116 234 0205**

THE BESSIE BLUE KILLER

Richard A. Lupoff

A film studio sets out to create a documentary about the Tuskegee Airmen, a unit of African-Americans who flew combat missions in World War Two — but filming has barely begun when a corpse is found on the set. Hobart Lindsey, insurance investigator turned detective, enters the scene, aided by Marvia Plum, his policewoman girlfriend. Soon he uncovers a mystery stretching half a century into the past — and suddenly and unexpectedly is flying through a hazardous murder investigation by the seat of his pants!

UNHOLY GROUND

Catriona McCuaig

When midwife Maudie Rouse marries the love of her life, policeman Dick Bryant, the pair could not be happier as they settle into contented domesticity in the village of Llandyfan. But troubles abound for the newlyweds — an abandoned baby, a difficult new district nurse, and the possibility of losing their home — and Maudie must find a way to deal with the problems, in addition to bicycling around the village performing her professional duties. Meanwhile, a grim discovery is made in a local farmer's field . . .